LITTLE DAISY
HISTORICAL VICTORIAN SAGA

❦

DOLLY PRICE

PUREREAD.COM

CONTENTS

Dear reader, get ready for another great story… 1
1. The Last Good Day 3
2. A Fatherless Family 13
3. With Papa Gone 24
4. Taking Care of the Family 35
5. Making Ends Meet 45
6. Girls Grow Up Fast 55
7. Back to the Mine 64
8. The Lesser Sin 74
9. Unwanted 83
10. Peril at the Market Place 94
11. The Lost Ones Meet 103
12. An Unlikely Family 113
13. The Complications of Marrying 125
14. The Wedding 136
15. The Past Returns 147
16. Alone 157
17. The Scullery Girl 165
18. A Visit with Uncle Ivor 173
19. Reunion 183
20. Introducing Jess Weir 193

Love Victorian Romance? 205
Our Gift To You 207

DEAR READER, GET READY FOR
ANOTHER GREAT STORY...

A VICTORIAN ROMANCE

Left to fend for herself and her five siblings, little Daisy Stanley works tirelessly to defend her family. But will the heavy hand of fate steal all of their futures?

Turn the page and let's begin

THE LAST GOOD DAY

"Come children," called Katherine as she handed her husband the lunch that she had packed for him. "Give Papa a kiss before he goes off to work."

The children lined up in order of their age, as they did every morning that Wilbur Stanley went to the mines to earn his living: six-year old Daisy, the eldest, with her dark plaits down her back; five-year old Gerald, who was, his mother claimed, the "dead spit" of Wilbur, with his black hair and cowlick and earnest dark eyes; plump four-year old Vera, the imp of the family; three-year old Eva, who followed Vera everywhere she went; two-year old Gus, intent on doing what his siblings did; and one year-old Morris, still in his mother's arms.

"Daisy, mind you kiss Papa extra special; it's your birthday today, remember! And we'll have a special supper for you tonight when Papa comes home," Mama said gaily.

Papa went down the line of his children and kissed each one. It was a ritual that he and his wife had begun when Daisy was old enough to stand on her own wobbly feet, for Katharine was ever mindful that going down into the mines was dangerous work. The children's kisses, she told Wilbur through the years as their family grew, would protect him from harm. Wilbur, the son, grandson, and great-grandson of miners, had never known anything but going down into the very guts of the earth, as he put it, to make a living. It didn't do to think too much on what that meant. But he indulged his wife and was happy to be blessed with kisses every morning. His wealth was in his family, and a morning that started off with their kisses made him a rich man. That was his creed and he thanked God every night for the abundance that he lived with in love. No matter that clothes were somewhat threadbare in places and the table sometimes sparse in food. The Stanleys were rich because they loved each other.

He kissed Daisy six times, one for each year of her life. "Now, see that you all behave for your mother," he said as he put on his miner's hat.

"Good-bye, Papa!" the children called as they stood at the front of the cottage to bid their father farewell as he joined the other men walking to the mines.

The men were not the only ones walking from the village. Some of the children were on their way to the school run by Dorothea Ames, a miner's widow whose mission it was to give the miners' children an education and a better life, one which would make them fit for work that did not require them to go down into the hidden depths of the earth and dig with their picks for the coal. Mrs. Ames had been left with nothing when her husband died: she had to move out of the small house where she had lived because those cabins were rented to miners, and she had little enough to take with her when she moved in with her widowed sister. But she knew how to read and write, and she vowed that the children of Oldham would know that much so that, one day, they could find better employment that didn't line their lungs with coal dust and didn't put them at risk every day of their lives.

Katherine did not allow Daisy to go to school. She was needed at home to help mind the children, Katherine said. Besides, it was bad luck, Katherine believed, to set children's minds to aspirations for which they were not suited.

But Daisy watched the children pass by, their schoolbooks and lunches in hand as they walked. Annie and Josephine, Daisy's friends, waved to her as they passed. Daisy waved back, and stayed at the door, watching until they were out of sight.

"Come inside now, Daisy, there's a good girl. See to the children getting their breakfast, won't you, while I feed Morris?"

"Mama, when will I be able to go to school?" It was not the first time she had asked that question, but she always hoped that one day, the answer would change.

Katherine pushed stray tendrils of her gilt blonde hair from her forehead. There was never time for a proper combing, it seemed, with six children to raise and a husband to look after. "School? What have the likes of us to do with schooling?" she scoffed. "It's enough that you're learning your letters and sums, isn't it? It's very good of your papa to take the time to teach you, and him tired from working all day when he comes home. Schooling is for those with time to spare."

Daisy didn't bother making the point that Annie's father worked in the mine as well as Papa, and Annie's mother had five children, or that Josephine's father was a widower whose sister tended to his family while he worked. She knew that her mother regarded schooling as frivolous. She often wondered what it would be like, knowing what all the words on a sign spelled, and knowing how to write one's own name so that others could read it. Papa could read and write, after a fashion, and he'd promised her that she'd learn as well. Papa said she was bright as the noonday sun, and she'd learn far more than he knew. Daisy was dubious at the comparison. In the mining town of Oldham,

England, the sun seemed very far away, blotted out by the smoke from the chimneys of the factories that were fueled by the coal that miners like Papa dug out of the ground.

There was no use thinking about reading and writing now, when she had the wee ones to look after while her mother tended to the baby. Daisy spooned oatmeal into bowls for Gerald, Vera, and Eva. She pulled Gus onto her lap. Gerald and Vera managed well enough on their own. Eva invariably ended up with as much oatmeal on her face as in her mouth. As Daisy made certain that they fed Eva, she listened to her brothers and sisters as their mother rarely had the time to do. The children enjoyed the morning chatter with their sister; despite the busy pace of the morning, Daisy made certain that each child, even little Gus, was part of the conversation. Baby Morris was a fussy child who demanded more of his mother's attention, which left her with less time or patience for the rest of her brood. Daisy was patient and encouraging, with never a raised voice or a cross word.

After the children had finished their oatmeal and Daisy had washed the bowls and spoons, she set them to their chores. Vera was given the task of drying the dishes that had just been washed. Eva, who was always at Vera's side, was also given a piece of toweling to dry them a second time. Gus was too small to work, and too big to ignore; Daisy told him that he could play with the wooden blocks that Papa had carved out of scraps of wood for Daisy six years ago. There wasn't money for toys, and what playthings they had were handed down.

Gerald was sent out to gather twigs and branches to use for firewood. Although the cottage was equipped with a coal stove, the coal itself had to be paid for, and whatever coal was bought came directly out of the miners' wagers. It wasn't winter yet, but winter came every year and Daisy minded what her father told her. "Put away now for what will be needed anon," he often said. "'Tis a wise steward who plans for the seven lean years, just as Joseph told the Pharoah to do back in Bible times."

Papa was full of Bible time stories and in the evenings, after the family had finished their supper and were gathered in the kitchen and around the table after it was cleared, he would tell them. Although he was not formally schooled except for the very basics, he had been a churchgoer from his youngest days, and he knew the scriptures like he knew the veins of coal in the ground. Then, after they'd had their stories and said their prayers, the youngest children would be sent off to bed. It was then that he would teach Daisy her letters and her sums.

Katherine thought such lessons to be a waste of time and she would usually go off to the bedroom that she and her husband shared, where she did the sewing and knitting and whatever mending needed to be attended to once Morris was asleep. This was Daisy's favorite time of the day, for unlike her mother, her father believed that learning, just as the Widow Ames asserted, was a way to a better life.

He had said, more than once, that he didn't want his own boys going into the ground to earn their bread. Nor did he want his daughters wedded to such as earned their living digging out the coal that the earth was none so eager to surrender. "'Tis a hard life, child," he'd told her often. "Hard on us what go down to dig out the coal, and hard on those what stay above the ground and fret. Your ma never ceases her fretting from the moment I'm out of sight in the morning until I come in the door in the evening. And then, the next day, she worries anew. No, 'tis not a life I want for you. You're a bright lass and a good one, and fair, too, though I ought not to say it, seeing as you and me, we're as like as two dark pieces of coal ourselves. But you learn what I can teach you, little enough though it is, and you pay heed to what I say. Look after your family and humble yourself before the Lord. You'll do all right."

Daisy was too young to understand what Papa meant by doing all right. She'd lived in Oldham, a mining village, all her life and all she knew was the coal; the dust that coated everything, inside and out when the stove was fueled with it; the prices at the company store that were higher, folks said, than what they ought to be because the mine owners turned a profit off the wares that were sold; the tired, slumped shoulders of the miners as they returned home from their shifts; the tired faces begrimed from the coal they'd wrested from the earth. Now and again, there was talk of a strike to force the owners to pay a fair wage, but no one paid much attention to the agitators, as the mine owners called them, who came round trying to stir up trouble. The miners didn't want trouble. They just wanted to feed their families.

Daisy knew, from Papa's words, that taking care of the family was the most important thing anyone could do, second only to paying due honor to the Lord. The family never missed church unless there was illness or when Katherine was in childbirth. They prayed on their knees every night before crawling into the beds where they slept, the three girls in one bed, Gerald and Gus in the other bed. Morris slept in his parents' bedroom, in his cradle on the floor next to their mother's side of the bed. He'd just begun crawling out of the cradle and he'd soon be moved to sharing the bed with his brothers. There didn't seem to be much time in between the period when the youngest moved into sleeping with siblings until Katherine was again expecting. It was the way of things. Daisy didn't question how things were. It was simply how they were, like church every Sunday and roast chicken for Christmas dinner and potato soup during lean times when Papa's wages didn't stretch for more.

Katherine came downstairs, tucking loose strands into her pinned hair.

"Is Baby asleep?" Daisy asked as she kneaded the dough that had been put to raise before breakfast.

Katherine nodded. "Poor mite, he fusses so after feeding. "Good girl," she said approvingly, noting her eldest daughter's progress with the bread baking. She tied an apron around her waist. "Your papa does so enjoy his bread and jam. I wish we had cherries for a pie. I'm fair starved for a piece of cherry pie."

Daisy gave her mother an evaluating look. Katherine laughed at the implied question in the glance. "'Tis too soon to be sure," she answered. "But the timing is right. I'd best get to weaning Morris."

Daisy wondered how the meager supply of food for the table would stretch to feed another mouth if Morris would no longer be fed at their mother's breast. But she said nothing. Newborn infants joining the family every year was another thing not to question. It just was how things were.

Katherine sat down at the table and began to cut up onions for supper. The girls, finished with drying the dishes, clamored to be allowed to go out and play. Katherine gave them an indulgent smile. "Take Gus with you," she directed them. "Stay out of the mud and don't let him get into the dirt."

The girls promised that they would do so and raced out of the house, leaving Daisy and her mother to work in the kitchen. Katherine chatted with Daisy about the sewing she planned to do, now that Daisy was growing. It wasn't often that Daisy and Katherine had time to talk together, and Daisy enjoyed the novelty of it. Katherine was explaining that she had a dress in her trunk that she was going to cut into cloth and make a new frock for Daisy. "'Tis time that you had a new dress," Katherine said. "Why, in another year or so, Vera will be fitting into your clothes. She's not as careful as you; I doubt there'll be anything to hand down to Eva—"

Noise from outside interrupted Katherine's sentence. She and Daisy shared a puzzled look before Katherine rose from her wooden chair. The noise was getting louder, and voices were raised. Someone screamed.

Katherine raced to the door, almost tripping in her haste. Daisy followed close behind. She saw Gerald running down the street, his cap precariously perched upon his dark hair as he hurried, gripping branches in his hand and waving them like signals.

"Daisy!" he called, shouting to be heard over the keening noise made by women who were already outside of their cottages and running in the direction of the mine. "The mine's caved in!"

A FATHERLESS FAMILY

Katherine grabbed hold of the door, but her knees buckled and she fell to the floor in a faint. Daisy was uncertain what to do: she couldn't leave their mother untended, but she needed to know more about what Gerald had said.

"Gerald," she said as she knelt down by her mother, whose eyes were closed. "Tell the girls to come inside. You find one of the women heading for the mine and ask her what's going on."

"Daisy," Gerald's lower lip was trembling. "Papa, is he in the mine?"

By now, Papa and all of the men on his shift would be in the mine. Daisy forced her thoughts away from the images that were brought to mind at the thought of a cave-in of the mine. Instead, she focused on what she needed to do. "Call the girls in and remind them to bring Gus with them. That scamp will be off running to play in all this ruckus. Then follow the folks on their way to the mine. You'll see Mrs. Larkin, Annie's ma, with the others. She'll tell you what's going on. Mind what she says, remember it, then come back here and tell me."

Gerald nodded, fortified by his sister's calm manner. "I'll be right back, Daisy," he promised as he scrambled out the door of the cabin. "Vera, Eva!" he bellowed. "Daisy says get inside and look sharp!"

"Mama," Daisy said softly as she took off her apron and, wadding it up, placed it underneath her mother's head. "Mama, you must rouse yourself. Baby Morris, he'll be wanting a feeding soon and you mustn't let him go hungry. Mama, please—"

Daisy caught herself before she allowed her next breath to turn into a sob. She didn't know what to do, and Mama wasn't herself, and Papa...

As if the thoughts in her head each occupied a separate room inside her mind, Daisy closed the door on the unthinkable possibility that Papa was buried alive in the mine, out of reach of any who could bring him above ground. That thought must not be allowed to leave the locked room where fearful notions stayed.

She and her brothers and sisters had kissed Papa that morning. Their kisses protected him from harm. Mama said so.

"Mama!" she raised her voice.

Vera came inside just then, Eva at her heels. "Why is Mama sleeping on the floor?" Vera wanted to know, more curious than concerned.

"She fell," Daisy answered briefly.

She lightly tapped her mother on the cheek.

"What for you hitting Mama?" Vera demanded as Eva stared owlishly at Daisy's strange behavior.

"I'm not hitting her, I'm trying to wake her," Daisy said.

"Looks like you're hitting her," Vera refuted Daisy. "Mama won't be pleased when she wakes to find you hitting her. Papa will hit you for it—Daisy, what was Gerald saying about the mine? Daisy, there's folks crying outside, I saw them. Why are they crying?"

"Vera, I don't know!" Daisy snapped. Then, instantly contrite, she softened her tone. "I'm sorry, Vera, lass, I didn't mean to speak harsh to you."

"I'll go find Gerald," Vera said importantly. "Me and Eva will find out where he's gone."

"No, you won't! You'll stay right here—where's Gus?"

Vera looked at Eva. Eva looked at Vera. "I don't know, Daisy," Vera replied. "I don't reckon he came in with us."

"Vera, you sit right here, right by Mama's side," Daisy said, standing up. "Eva, you sit on Mama's other side. Don't go anywhere, you hear me?"

"Do I have to hit Mama like you were doing?" Vera asked as she obeyed her sister's order.

"I wasn't hitting—no, don't hit her!" Daisy realized the futility of trying to explain to her inquisitive younger sister that she was merely trying to rouse their mother out of what was a strange sleep. "Just stay by her side."

"Where are you going" Vera asked.

Daisy took her shawl down from the wooden rack on the wall and wrapped it around her shoulders. "I'm going to find out why everyone is going to the mine."

"Daisy, don't leave us," Vera begged. The little girl's round blue eyes were on the brink of shedding tears. "Don't leave us alone!"

Daisy bent down to kiss her sister's cheek. "You aren't alone," she said. "Mama is here."

Vera was not reassured. "Mama won't wake. Is Mama dead, Daisy?"

"No! She's—she fell. She fell in a faint. She'll be fine when she comes round, don't fear. But if she wakes up and no one is nearby, she'll be frightened, wondering where everyone has gone. Stay by her side. Do you hear me? Stay there."

Aware that she'd already lost valuable time in which Gus could have wandered off in any direction, Daisy ran out the door, closing it behind her. She knew that her sisters were frightened by what they could not understand, but Gus had to be found. He was too young to be wandering off on his own. The town was a small one and folks knew one another, but there were countless ways in which a child the age of Gus could get himself into peril. He could be trampled by a horse or fall into a well. He could be captured by gypsies and never seen again. He could be taken for an orphan and put in the foundling home. The half-understood conversations of adults that Daisy had overheard in her short lifetime managed to stitch themselves together like a cloak of peril and she could not divest herself of the fears.

"Mrs. Larkin!" she called out, spotting Annie's mother in the street, carrying one child in her arms and holding another by the hand. "What's happened at the mine?"

Mrs. Larkin stopped. "Bless us, child, I'm on my way to find out. Thanks be to God that my Herbert isn't working the morning shift; he's—" she stopped, seeing the stricken look on Daisy's face. "There, there now, no reason to fear on what we don't know, is there?" she said in a consoling voice as she took the edge of her apron to wipe away the early drops of tears that were trickling from Daisy's eyes. "Now, now—where's your ma?"

"Ma fainted, ma'am, when she heard Gerald say the mine caved in. Vera and Eva are watching her now. Gerald went to the mine to find out what he can. I'm looking for Gus."

"Merciful God, you don't mean he's gone off by himself, Daisy. Come now, child, we'll find him." Mrs. Larkin, immediately directed to the more pressing concern, hoisted her youngest higher on her hip. "Lucy, you hold Daisy's hand, now," she said.

Daisy was relieved that an adult was coming to her aid, but she didn't want to impose upon Annie's mother. "Ma'am, I'm very grateful to you," she said. "Didn't you mean to go to the mine?"

"Bless us, child, but it's more important to find that little boy. In a few moments, these streets will be crowded with folks from the mine, trying to find out what's happening. And what they'll need to get out of paying for," she muttered under her breath. "I'd not want that wee boy to be wandering lost in the midst of the confusion that's like to fall upon us."

"Why will folks be coming?" Daisy asked, puzzled by Mrs. Larkin's words.

"There'll be the men from the newspaper," Mrs. Larkin said bitterly, "wanting to write about the cave-in. Disaster, that's what they'll call it, and so it is. There will be the toffs, you know, the ones in their suits and their clean hands, wondering how much money they're losing while the mine can't operate because the men are trapped inside

—oh, child," she said, halting her rush of words at the expression on Daisy's face. "It's not my intention to put fear into you." She exhaled. "But you might as well know the truth about mining. It's against nature to be digging so deep below the ground that at any moment a man's ax might strike the wall that separates us from the Devil's lair. There's nothing good comes of a mine cave-in. Good men die and widows are left with orphaned children. And no compensation from those what own the mines, you can be sure of that. Not even time to grieve before the family has to move out of the cabins that are rented to the miners. Oh, child," Mrs. Larkin exclaimed in a burst of anger mingled with sorrow, her usually pleasant, freckled face contorted in dismay, "'a mine cave-in is a bad business for all! Now, come along and we'll find that wee brother of yours. There's enough sadness for today without anything adding more to it."

∽

By the time they found Gus, sitting by himself in a field, pulling up wildflowers with his chubby fingers, watching in wonder as the streets of the town filled with people, Mrs. Larkin's words had come to pass. Daisy saw strangers hurrying past with an impression of great purpose. Men on horseback, impatient at being impeded by the throngs of people around them, cursed as their pace was slowed by the human obstacles in their way. At one point, however, a carriage, led by a team of smart-looking chestnuts moving with a brisk and businesslike step, appeared and then, the people moved to the sides so that the vehicle could pass without encumbrance.

Mrs. Larkin's lips thinned. "Him!" she said with a sniff.

Daisy wondered what she meant. "Who is he?" she asked curiously. She was holding onto Gus with one firm hand, determined not to let him go. Mrs. Larkin had once again taken charge of both her children while keeping a close eye on the Stanley children huddled close to her ample skirts.

"Mr. Olsen," Mrs. Larkin replied.

Daisy didn't know who Mr. Olsen was. A note in Mrs. Larkin's voice revealed that he was not someone in the woman's favor, but he was not someone she could disregard either.

"Who is Mr. Olsen?"

Mrs. Larkin turned her head and gave Daisy a look of surprise. "You don't know who Mr. Olsen is?" she said.

Daisy shook her head. She tugged on Gus's hand; he had seen the carriage pass by and wanted to follow it.

"He owns the mine, child," Mrs. Larkin said. She sighed. "Which is to say, he owns us all."

Daisy didn't understand what that meant. She had never heard her parents mention the name of Mr. Olsen. Nor had anyone ever told her that she was owned by someone whose name, until today, was unknown to her. She supposed that her parents owned her; she was their daughter and the Bible said she owed them obedience. She supposed that was the same as being owned by them. Mama put the meals on the table, bought with money that Papa earned as a miner. They had clothing, worn, to be sure, but clean. They had a home in which to live. Did Mr. Olsen own all of those things as well?

It was too much to consider, and more than her mind could absorb. She did not know where Gerald had gone to, but she was not worried. Her five-year old brother was cautious and would not get into trouble. Daisy was certain of this. Gus was too young to understand that he mustn't wander; Vera mainly obeyed instructions although she questioned their purpose and Eva followed Vera. Morris wasn't old enough to get into mischief on his own.

As they neared the Stanley cabin, Daisy remembered her manners. "Thank you, ma'am," she said politely, "for taking the time to help me find Gus. I'm very sorry to have troubled you."

"Bless you, child," Mrs. Larkin said and, to Daisy's astonishment, the woman released her young daughter's hand for a moment to bring her shawl to her eyes and wipe a tear away. "Growed up too soon, I shouldn't wonder, and now likely to grow even faster. I'll come in with you and see to your mam."

"She fell," Daisy supplied, the lie coming readily to her lips. For some reason that she could not fathom, Mrs. Larkin seemed to be critical of Mama because Gus had wandered off. She was only slightly appeased when Daisy said that Mama had fallen and that Vera and Eva were looking after her. It was true that Daisy could not imagine Mrs. Larkin succumbing to a fall at such a time, but she felt that she needed to protect her mother from the disapproval of others.

Mrs. Larkin didn't answer, but as she walked the last few steps to the cabin, she traveled the distance to the door with a formidable step.

Daisy opened the door. Mama was seated at the kitchen table, her head buried in her hands as she howled in grief. Vera and Eva, perplexed, stood beside her with upturned faces, uncertain of what to do. Vera, seeing Daisy, looked relieved.

"Daisy, Morris is crying and crying. We think he's hungry. I told Mama, but she doesn't hear me."

Mrs. Larkin handed the baby in her arms to Daisy. "Lucy, you stay right where you are," she said to her other daughter. She went up to the table and took hold of Katherine's wrist firmly. "Now, you must look to your children, Katherine," she said. "They need you."

"I need Wilbur!" Katherine cried out. "I need him, and he's dead in a mine and no help to anyone now!"

Dead? Eva and Vera looked to Daisy. They knew what dead meant.

Daisy looked away. She wished Mama would stop crying and tell them all what had happened to Papa.

"He's dead!" Katherine wailed. "What shall we do? What's to become of us!"

WITH PAPA GONE

When Katherine learned that there could be no burial of her husband, or of the other men who had died in the collapsed mine, she was overcome with grief and took to her bed. When Daisy, after she had made supper and fed the children and listened to their prayers before they went to sleep, went to check on her mother, she saw the red stain that was spreading across the bedlinens where Katherine lay.

"Mama!" Daisy cried out, horrified by the sight and perplexed at its source. "You are ailing!"

Mama moaned and clutched at her belly. "The baby," she wept. "I'm losing it. First Wilbur and now his child . . . you children, you failed me. Your kisses were to protect your poor Papa. You did not love him enough!"

"Mama?" Daisy queried. "What do you mean?" Was Mama dying?

Mama's face was very pale, but her eyes burned as if they were heated by the coal that Papa and the other miners dug from the ground. "I wish I was dying," she spat out the words in a violent sob. "I should be dead with him. Leave you children to the mercy of the orphanage and give me peace!" A spasm of pain seized her, and she gripped her belly. "You did not give him all your love this morning! You held back! I know you did. Selfish children, thinking of your breakfast, you of that school you so wanted to go to. See how you are punished? Your good Papa, who taught you what he knew, is now dead in the ground, denied a Christian burial! You will learn no more, it's punishment for your selfishness!"

"Mama," Daisy cried. Her mother's words slashed at her with the sharpness of cooking knives. How could Mama say such terrible things? How could Daisy have prevented the mine from collapsing? "Mama, I loved Papa!"

"Oh, yes, you loved him," Katherine seethed. "You loved him more than me, I knew it, I always knew it. You took the time that should have been mine so that he could teach you your letters and sums. Much good that will do you now. You'll be off to work, my girl, earning wages for this family. You failed your Papa; you shan't fail the rest of us!"

The blood on the front of Mama's blue dress was scarlet and fresh. Daisy knew that she had to seek help. What if Mama should die? What would happen to them?

"I'll bring Mrs. Larkin," she said hastily and ran out of the room and out of the house before Katherine could began another rant.

She ran the distance to the Larkin home. The street was silent as if in observation of the grieving that was taking place behind the doors of the cabins. Not all cabins were filled with families who had lost fathers and husbands, but in the small mining community, grief was the thread that tied them together. What happened today would happen again; mining families knew it.

The door to the Larkin cabin opened almost as soon as Daisy knocked. Mrs. Larkin looked down upon Daisy. "Child," she said quietly.

"It's Mama," Daisy said, drawing gasping breaths from racing down the street in such haste. "She's bleeding, she says she's losing the baby, she says it's my fault—"

"Herbert, I'm going to the Stanleys," Mrs. Larkin called over her shoulder as she grabbed her shawl and then closed the door. Before the door closed, Daisy saw Annie, along with her brothers and sisters, sitting around the table with their father.

Annie had her family still. Her day had not been ripped apart by the collapse of the mine. Her life was unchanged. Daisy's face crumpled. How could it be that this terrible thing had happened to the Stanleys? Was Mama right? Was it the fault of Daisy and her brothers and sisters? Had they failed Papa? Mama had always stressed to her children that they must send Papa off in the morning with all their love. But it had not been enough and now he was in the mine forever.

"Daisy," Mrs. Larkin took Daisy's hand as they walked. "Your ma is grieving. You must take no mind of what she says. She's lost her man and she's feeling lost herself. If she was carrying a child, well, she's not the first woman to lose a baby early on. I reckon it's addled her a bit and no wonder."

"She said I'll need to go to work to take care of the family," Daisy said. She didn't know what Mama meant. How could Daisy earn a living? She couldn't go down into the mines. What could she hope to do that would bring in the money they would need for food, for the rent for the miner's cabin where they lived, for all that they needed?

"Aye, well, that's the way of it now. The factories, they're keen on hiring children to do the work that needs doing. A pity of it, but your ma spoke true when she said that."

They had reached the cabin. Mama's sobs could be heard through the open window of the cabin. Mrs. Larkin, who had been bent over to talk to Daisy, straightened. "Times like this, child, they test us. How your ma will go on from here will tell whether she's one who breaks or one who bends."

Daisy didn't understand what Mrs. Larkin meant but there was no time to ask. Mrs. Larkin opened the door and went inside.

All the cabins were built with the same layout, which made it easy for Mrs. Larkin to know in which direction to go to find Katherine. Daisy followed Mrs. Larkin into the bedroom.

Mama was writhing on the bed, sobbing and muttering. Her silver blonde hair was loose and tousled upon the pillow and her face was very pale.

"Now, Katherine," Mrs. Larkin addressed Mama in a matter-of-fact tone, "You're having a right bad time of it and no mistake. Nature has to take its course now until 'tis over. I'll stay here with you."

"I want to be with Wilbur!" Mama wailed, grabbing Mrs. Larkin's wrist. "I want to be in the ground with him. He can't even be given a Christian burial," she said as she raised herself up on her elbow. "The mine is his grave! It's unhallowed ground!"

"Daisy, bring me a basin of water, and clean cloths," Mrs. Larkin said in the same brisk tone she had used with Mama.

"It's her fault!" Katherine shrieked. Her lovely hair was now a tangle framing the wild-eyed features. "She failed her Papa!"

"Katherine," Mrs. Larkin said in a voice that brooked no nonsense. "This child had nothing to do with the mine collapse. She's a good girl and she needs you to be strong now—Daisy, go on now and get that water. Then you can go off to bed. This is no business for a child your age." Under her breath, Mrs. Larkin added, "You'll come to it soon enough, as every woman does."

Daisy didn't understand that either, but she gave it no thought. She was simply relieved to have an adult present who knew how to handle Mama and knew what to do about the bleeding. Daisy didn't understand that, one of the many things she was finding that were beyond her understanding now that Papa was gone and Mama didn't seem to be herself.

She checked on the little ones, making sure that they were in bed, just as they were supposed to be. Gerald had thought to bring baby Morris into the boys' bed. His arm was draped protectively over his youngest brother.

When Mrs. Larkin emerged from the bedroom where Mama was, she saw Daisy waiting patiently at the kitchen table.

Daisy noticed that the water in the basin was tinged red. "Is Mama dead?" Daisy asked. In this day of loss, she wondered if perhaps Death was on the loose and if she was now an orphan. It didn't seem possible that Papa would not come in through the door, eager for his supper and his kisses from his children. Daisy didn't understand that either.

"No, child. Your ma is sleeping now. I gave her a nip of something to make her sleep through the night." Mrs. Larkin went to the door, opened it, and dumped the water outside. "You need to get your rest, child. You've got a hard lot ahead of you. Your ma . . . she's going to depend on you a lot, though you but a child and she a grown woman."

There was a note of criticism in Mrs. Larkin's words. Daisy wasn't sure what that meant, or who Mrs. Larkin was criticizing. Was she critical of Daisy?

"I'll be by in the morning after mine get off to school," Mrs. Larkin said.

The children were very somber the next morning when they gathered at the table for oatmeal. Vera didn't understand why Papa hadn't come home, and Eva, who copied everything Vera did, cried as well with the questions.

Gerald looked at Daisy, his somber face even more grave. "Daisy, Papa . . . he's not coming home, is he?"

Daisy knew she had to be strong. Papa would want to her be strong. He would expect her to take care of her family. "Papa is in heaven," she said bravely. "He loves us and he's looking down upon us, so we must be very good. We shall have to look after Mama and baby Morris so that we don't let Papa down."

"How did he get to heaven?" Vera wanted to know, "if he's in the mine?"

Having questions to ask diverted Vera from her tears. Vera liked asking questions. It was tiresome at times, trying to answer them, but the questions she was asking now were ones for which Daisy had no answers. "I don't know how he got there," Daisy said honestly. "I suppose the angels took him there."

Vera was appeased by this response. To be transported by angels was a pleasant thought. "He's not coming home to us?"

Daisy shook her head. "No. but he's in our hearts, remember that. He is watching us every minute."

"Doesn't he sleep in heaven?"

"Angels don't sleep," Gerald supplied the answer, with some scorn. How could angels sleep when they had wings.

"Don't they get tired?" Vera went on.

"No," Gerald said, but he looked to Daisy with uncertainty, as if she would know more.

That was when Daisy knew that, in some unfathomable way, she was no longer a child. She was still six years old, but birthdays didn't matter. Papa was dead and Mama was ill, and it was up to Daisy to take care of the family. How she was going to do that, she didn't know.

∼

Mrs. Larkin found them lodgings with Sadie Calloway, a sailor's widow who had lost her husband not to the mines, but to the sea. Sadie wasn't dependent upon the Olsens for a place to live because her husband had bought a little house on the outskirts of the village, closer to the textile factory than to the mine. She had rooms to let, and her rates were reasonable. Knowing that the Stanleys had no income, Mrs. Calloway said that Daisy and Gerald could help her with chores in exchange for renting the one room where all of them were to board until, Mrs. Calloway said, Katherine was up to finding a position in the mill.

Mrs. Larkin helped them pack, but that didn't take long. They owned surprisingly little for a family of six that had lived in the crowded cabin all their lives. When Daisy asked how they would manage to find space in the single room where they would be living to house the cooking pots, the plates and cups, the bedlinens, the wooden toys that Papa had carved for them, the trunk filled with outgrown clothing that Mama used to make new garments for the children as they grew, Mrs. Larkin's advice was simple.

"Some things can be sold," she said. "You'll need money at times, and you can sell a pot for a few shillings. While you're living at Sadie Calloway's, you won't need to cook your own food. She includes one meal a day with the boarding fee. The little ones will play with the toys. Sometimes, child, you must needs turn your mind to what you need to do. Until your ma comes around to her own senses, that is."

Mrs. Larkin sounded dubious about when this would happen. Daisy's thoughts echoed the older woman's thinking. Mama seemed to sleep all day and night, with no interest in her children or what was to become of the family. That put the responsibility on Daisy's six-year-old shoulders.

"There's one more thing, child, though I feel shame at bringing it up to a girl your age," Mrs. Larkin halted as she rested the pushcart that she had wheedled out of a neighbor for the Stanleys to use for their move.

Daisy didn't ask questions. She paused beside Mrs. Larkin. Up ahead, Gerald was shepherding his sisters. The two younger boys were in the pushcart along with the family's belongings, intrigued at this means of travel.

Mrs. Larkin looked off into the distance. Up ahead was the textile mill, a large building that dominated the landscape above ground as much as the mine owned the territory below the town. "Sadie Calloway, well, she's a good sort. Got a kind heart on her. But she has to make a living, see, and she knows sailors from when her man was one. Sometimes, when they come ashore, they know they'll find a hot meal and a warm bed at Sadie's."

This did not seem so unusual to Daisy. If Mrs. Calloway managed a boarding house, then she would have boarders. It was perfectly clear to Daisy and made her wonder why Mrs. Larkin thought this was something difficult to explain to a six-year-old.

"Sailors, they're not like miners. They're away from home for a long stretch of time. Weeks, months. They like seeing a pretty face when they're off the ship."

Daisy's small face showed puzzlement, but she said nothing, waiting for Mrs. Larkin to explain. Sometimes, she had found, adults were slow to say what they meant.

"Your ma, she's a pretty woman. Some of the sailors . . . Daisy, child, I hope I haven't steered you amiss by sending you to Sadie's. It's better than the streets, and the Olsens wouldn't care if they turned your family out with nowhere to go. They've done it before. I only pray that your ma doesn't go wrong. But if she does, child, you stay by the right. You know the commandments and you know the difference between right and wrong. You won't let your family down," Mrs. Larkin said fiercely, bending down so that she and Daisy were at eye level. "You won't be a child forever, you know. You do what you know is right now. Take care of your family, and when you're a woman grown, you make the right choices. Don't marry a miner, Daisy, it's a lifetime of fear. Some women, the ones like your ma, they don't know how to manage. But you've got an old head on those young shoulders. Stay strong in God and you'll do your pa proud."

TAKING CARE OF THE FAMILY

In the two years since Papa's death had changed the Stanley family forever, Daisy had come to understand more of what Mrs. Larkin had meant by her parting words. Sadie Calloway was a genial woman with a ready smile, and she was kind enough to keep an eye on the younger Stanleys when Mama was too tired to do so.

Mama was often tired in the daytime because she was keeping company with the sailors who came ashore looking for what Sadie explained was companionship. Daisy didn't understand why Mama was ready to oblige the sailors seeking companionship by accompanying them to the nearby pub. The children had gotten used to being home alone at night. It was Daisy who tucked them in at night before she went downstairs to clean up after the evening meal. Mrs. Calloway was generally at the pub along with Mama and the sailors and she often said what a help Daisy was.

It was Daisy, not Mrs. Calloway, who was up before dawn to stir coal into the stoves so that she could make breakfast, and it was Daisy who heated the water for washing dishes. Daisy washed the clothes of the lodgers, who paid Mrs. Calloway extra for the service. Daisy baked bread every day and went into the village to purchase food for meals, paying close attention to the cost of everything so that when the merchants sent their bills to Mrs. Calloway, Daisy could refute a cost if it was not accurate. The Oldham merchants soon learned that they could not cheat the little girl with the solemn face and the long black braids.

Daisy had not forgotten her dream of going to school, but there was no time for school now. Taking care of the family was her responsibility and she did not shirk her duty. She was just as attentive on Sunday morning, making sure that her siblings washed thoroughly on Saturday night and were properly dressed on Sunday morning so that they could attend services. They walked to church, and they walked back, but no one complained. Daisy told them this was what Papa wanted them to do and the children obeyed.

When Vera asked why Mama didn't go to church with them, if that was what Papa wanted, Daisy said that Mama was tired in the morning. But it didn't take long for the children to realize that their mother's late evenings at the pub were the reason she was tired in the morning. When Vera asked why Mama stayed out so late at night, Daisy didn't know what to say. When Vera asked why there were men coming home with Mama late at night, Daisy knew that she had to find a solution to what was an increasingly uncomfortable situation.

She saw the Larkins every Sunday in church, but when Mrs. Larkin asked how she was doing, Daisy politely replied that they were doing well. Mrs. Larkin seemed to understand Daisy's dilemma, because she sighed and hugged her and said no more.

Gerald had become her confidant because there was no one else Daisy could go to with these confounding problems. One night, after the younger children had had their supper and were in bed and sound asleep, Daisy and Gerald sat together on the front steps of the boarding house. Summer, with its lingering daylight and warmth, made it possible for the two of them to be comfortable outside. Mama and Mrs. Calloway had gone to the pub, as was their habit of nights, and several others of the boarders were away as well.

The children could have sat at the dining table to talk, but Daisy preferred the privacy of the outdoors. From where they sat, they could hear the noise coming from inside the pub; they could hear the rowdy songs and the laughter floating out through the open windows. Sometimes they heard Mama singing; these were not the hymns that she had sung in their home while she took care of the baby or cooked meals. They didn't understand the words, or why the lyrics seemed to inspire such rousing bursts of laughter from the others in the pub.

Daisy knew something was not right. But she couldn't identify the problem. She had given it much thought and now that she was eight, she had come up with what she thought might be a solution. She shared that decision with Gerald, who was, like his sister, sober and responsible.

"I went to the textile mill today," she told him, "on my way back from the butcher shop."

"Why?" Gerald wanted to know.

"We need to have two rooms," Daisy said. "Mrs. Calloway lets us rent one room in exchange for you and me working for her. If we earned proper wages, we could afford to rent a second room for Mama."

Daisy didn't need to explain why their mother needed her own room. Gerald knew. Sometimes, the drunken sailors who came home with her at night were loud and they woke up the children. The room was too small, and too crowded. Daisy refrained from offering details of which Gerald was already aware.

People passing by on their way to the pub didn't notice the two children sitting on the steps of the boarding house. They were intent on gaiety and a good time, and Daisy and Gerald did nothing to attract attention. Daisy kept her ears attentive to the open window on the second floor, lest the children, her siblings, were awakened by noise. But the Stanley children had adapted to the change in routine. Their home was much different, and Mama was very different, and Papa was gone. But Daisy was just the same as she always was, patient and attentive, and so, after a while, they had come to accept this altered way of living.

Daisy had no way of changing the circumstances, but earning wages and being able to afford a second room so that Mama could provide companionship, as Mrs. Larkin had delicately phrased it, without exposing the children to the sordid nature of that companionship, seemed to be what Papa would have wanted Daisy to do.

"Morris and Gus are too young to work, but you and me, and Vera and Eva, we could have jobs. The man I spoke to at the mill said he'd hire all of us."

Daisy decided not to share her impressions of the man who had provided her with the information regarding employment.

"You'll all do your work if you expect to be paid," he'd said curtly, his face encircled by the foul-smelling smoke from the cigar in his mouth. "No talking, no being late, no falling asleep on the job. The little ones, their job is to pick up the pieces of cotton under the machines. They'll need to be quick or they're like to get caught up in the machinery. Might die that way or lose a finger. An older one like you, you'll be standing at a loom all day. Don't whine that you're tired or your legs hurt. You'll do your job, or you'll get sacked. Work starts at six o'clock in the morning and the day ends at eight o'clock at night. Don't blather that you're tired; if you're old enough to take on a job, you'll do it without complaining."

He hadn't been particularly friendly, but Daisy had not expected anything else. She had learned that adults were not all like Mrs. Larkin, mindful of a child's needs. But without a father, and with their mother as she now was, the Stanley children had no other option. They had to earn wages.

"I don't think we'll be particularly happy working in the textile factory," Daisy admitted to her brother.

"We're not especially happy now," Gerald said bluntly. Like his older sister, Gerald was pragmatic. What options did they have? "How will you tell Mrs. Calloway?"

"I'll tell her that with wages, we'll pay her enough to rent two rooms."

"What about our suppers? We're fed now."

"One meal is included in the rent."

"Meals for all of us?" Gerald pressed.

The door of the pub opened, and a sailor emerged with one of the female boarders on his arm.

"Let's go inside," Daisy urged.

Gerald didn't need to be persuaded. The brother and sister hurried back into the boarding house. They had finished their discussion. Now it was up to Daisy to deliver her decision to Mrs. Calloway.

Their landlady was not at all pleased with the news, even at the prospect of being paid wages.

"I've beggared myself to provide for you children," Mrs. Calloway lamented. "Daisy, girl, fetch me a cold cloth for me head. I've a dreadful, thumping headache."

Obediently Daisy did as she was bade and handed the cloth to Mrs. Calloway, who pressed it against her forehead. "I'm plagued by miseries of all sorts and now you tell me that you want to work in the cotton mills. Have you any notion of what it's like in there? It's hot in the summer and cold in the winter; you'll catch pneumonia and die of it, I shouldn't wonder," she predicted lugubriously. "It's the children do the dangerous work, you know, running under the machines to fix the threads what break, or cleaning. There's bits of cotton everywhere, I hear. So much that it gets into your lungs. They tell me there are laws against children as young as you and your brothers and sisters working, but it don't look to me like anyone is enforcing those laws. It's children I see leaving the mill when the day is over. Children and women."

Mrs. Calloway pushed back the strands of brassy yellow hair that had gotten wet from the cloth covering her forehead. "You want to leave here, where I treat you like a princess, to go to the mill where you'll be treated worse than a slave?"

"No, Mrs. Calloway. We're very grateful for all that you do for us. But it's not fair to you. We should be paying our way. It's what our Papa would have expected." Daisy had carefully worked out the words she would use to convince Mrs. Calloway that having the Stanley children work at the mill would be to her benefit. "And we need to rent a second room. For our mother."

Daisy met Mrs. Calloway's gaze squarely. It was the other woman who looked away in embarrassment. "Yes, well, I suppose . . . that is, it would be better if Katherine had a room of her own. She is an adult, after all."

Daisy had put the kettle on the stove. As the whistling steam announced that the water was boiling, she poured a cup for Mrs. Calloway, steeping the leaves with her usual precise timing. She put sugar into the tea and handed it to the older woman, who breathed in the aroma gratefully.

"I reckon we can come to an arrangement," Mrs. Calloway said as she handed the cloth to Daisy to be refreshed. "What about the boys?" she demanded suddenly. "Your sisters won't be here to mind them."

The fact that Mrs. Calloway did not even suggest that Katherine should be watching her own little boys was not lost on Daisy.

"Gus is four now," Daisy said. "He doesn't take much minding anymore. He stays out of trouble, and he doesn't bother anyone. Morris is three now. If you can keep them downstairs with you, I don't think they'll need much minding. In exchange for you looking after them, Gerald will continue to keep the fireplaces clean, and I will do the dishes when I come home."

It was a very good arrangement, Daisy knew. Her little brothers would play quietly together and would listen to Mrs. Calloway. They would also be handy in taking care of small chores, such as sweeping the floors and other general housekeeping tasks that the indolent Mrs. Calloway neglected. Despite their tender years, they had absorbed some of their oldest sister's willingness to work, and they never grumbled when asked to lend a hand. Mrs. Calloway, childless herself, had a soft spot for the youngest Stanleys and rewarded them with sweets when they helped her. Daisy knew that the boys would be looked after and even loved, after a fashion, by Mrs. Calloway. It was a sad truth that the landlady provided the boys with more affection than their own mother had time to give them, but Daisy could do nothing about that.

All that she could do was to earn wages. Someday, she would be an adult and she would be able to provide more of what her family needed. Now what they needed most was to be shielded from their mother's dissolute ways. Working at the mill would enable Daisy to pay rent for two rooms but could not preserve the innocence of the Stanley children. But it would, Daisy felt, be what Papa would have wanted for his children.

MAKING ENDS MEET

Working at the mill and earning wages did not solve all the problems the Stanley children faced. When their mother discovered that they were earning money, she demanded that they turn their wages over to her. Every week, Daisy was faced with the equal dilemmas of having enough money to pay Mrs. Calloway the rent money that was owed to her and giving Katherine what she demanded. But the money that went to Katherine ended up being spent at the pub.

The children were tired at the end of their working days. They labored without complaint as they had learned to do. Vera and Eva were nimble and, warned by Daisy not to dawdle but to pick up the stray bits of cotton as quickly as they could or risk losing a finger, they wasted no time in keeping their areas clean. Gerald was a piecer at the mill, tasked with repairing the threads that broke during the spinning process. Daisy, because she assiduously worked steadily and skillfully, was made a bobbin girl soon after she started, running from the looms to replace empty bobbins with full ones in order for the weaving to continue.

Sundays were welcome days for the children. On Saturday nights, they had their weekly baths so that they were clean for church. They didn't mind the two-mile walk to church in the pleasant weather, for the farther from the mill they walked, the more they appreciated the open air, the fragrance of the bounty of nature and her many different perfumes, and the sheer delight of being out-of-doors. It was not so in the cold, wet months, when they walked to church with their heads bent against the rain or snow, their outer clothing insufficient to ward off the chill and the wind.

Mrs. Larkin, moved to pity by the Stanley children's diligence, had set herself and her daughters to knitting so that, even if the weather was bad, the children had scarves and gloves to wear.

Daisy appreciated Mrs. Larkin's thoughtfulness. She only wished that she could reciprocate the kindness. But there was no money left by the time the rent was paid and Katherine had taken what she regarded as due to her.

It was autumn now, and while the sun was still warm on their backs as they walked home from church, the children dreaded the onset of winter. It was no use asking if they could stay home on the coldest days, or when it was snowing or raining, for Daisy simply said that Papa expected them to go to church every Sunday, as they would have done if he had been with them.

They walked slowly as they were on their way back to the boarding house. Katherine would still be asleep, they knew. Mrs. Calloway would be looking for them to return so that Daisy could prepare the evening meal and Eva and Vera could do the washing up, while Gerald cleaned the fireplaces in the rooms. Gus and Morris would help wherever they could.

As Daisy listened to her siblings chatter, she had no time to appreciate the brilliant hues of the leaves on the trees, or to savor the still-warm sunshine that allowed them to walk without shivering. She had another matter on her mind.

She had learned that the law required young children who worked in the mills to be provided with schooling. One hour a week for learning! It seemed like a miracle. Daisy knew that she couldn't avail herself of the opportunity, she needed to produce every bit of earnings that she could. But she wanted Gerald, Vera, and Eva to get an education in some way so that, by the time they were old enough to live on their own, they would know how to read and write.

Daisy had gained an education of sorts by learning to read the shopping lists that Mrs. Calloway had written when she sent her to the stores to buy food and supplies. Daisy had learned a basic knowledge of arithmetic from the portions of meat and vegetables that she purchased, and how much was paid for them. It was not what she would have liked, but it was furthering the lessons that her father had given her before he died. Daisy wanted that for her siblings.

The dilemma arose from the fact that an hour of schooling each week for each child meant that four hours of wages a week would be lost. They were barely able to manage the rent and Katherine's demands now. How would they be able to muster the needed funds if they were deficient by four hours a week?

She had to bring the matter up to the children. If they were unwilling and she could not persuade them, Daisy knew that her efforts would be in vain.

When they reached the apple orchard that was halfway between the church and home, Daisy suddenly turned around to face her siblings. They looked at her in surprise; they were in no great hurry to return home, but it was usually Daisy, mindful of the work she needed to do to placate Mrs. Calloway, who urged them on.

"I want you to learn to read and write," she announced without preamble.

The sweet and tart aromas of the ripening apples filled their nostrils. Apples were a luxury they could not afford except when Daisy managed to wrest a few coins from the amount that she was forced to give to Katherine. The spreading branches of the trees provided a tantalizing scented canopy over their heads. Reading and writing were the farthest things from their minds.

Until Daisy, inspired, said, "If you get an education now, you'll all be able to work at better jobs when you're grown up. You'll be able to afford treats like apples in season. And two meals a day," she added artfully, knowing that they were all hungry for most of the day unless they had enough strength of will at their evening meals to put aside a piece of bread to eat in the morning before leaving for the textile mill.

Vera licked her lips as if she could taste the bites of apple just from breathing in their scent. "Imagine having apples whenever we wanted them," she said.

"And meat pies," said Eva, who found the odors of the vendors and their wares unbearably enticing when walking home from the mill each day.

"I suppose we could manage an hour," Gerald said, sounding pessimistic. He knew what a battle his sister fought each week in order to be able to afford their rent and their mother's nightly drinking at the pub. Now that she had the money from their earnings, she spent even more time at the pub than she had before her children were employed at the mill. He gave his sister a sideways glance. "Can we?" he asked as if he doubted his own answer.

"We'll have to," Daisy said, sounding sure when she was not at all sure. "It's what Papa would have wanted."

What Papa would have wanted was, they all knew, the deciding factor in any conclusion for Daisy. Eva barely remembered her father and depended upon Vera to refresh her memory. The two youngest boys had no memory of Papa at all. Daisy and Gerald remembered him and spared no opportunity to share their recollections. For Daisy, it was a mission as important as doing what he wanted. His death did not diminish his importance to the family, not in Daisy's view.

When the children arrived back at the boarding house, they immediately set to work on their chores. Daisy opened the door to the room where Katherine slept: her mother was sound asleep, and alone. Daisy quietly shut the door.

Mrs. Calloway, bleary-eyed from the indulgence of the night, yawned when Daisy came into the kitchen. "The boys have been angels," she said. "They're down for naps now. I think I'll have one meself. Bert gave me a good price on the beef I bought yesterday. It's likely to go off in a day or so, so you can cook it for supper tonight." She waved a hand at the pantry shelves. "As for the rest, you figure out what to make. You're the cook."

Daisy was in somewhat of a celebratory mood as she cut vegetables and rolled dough for the meal. Knowing that Gerald, Vera, and Eva were amenable to having an hour of schooling buoyed her confidence. This was what Papa would have wanted for his children. With learning, they could aspire to more than the long hours of the mill, with its alternating scenarios of danger and drudgery. When she saw that among Mrs. Calloway's purchases was a sack of apples, slightly wrinkled and, like the beef, not quite at their best but still acceptable for eating, she felt as if God had sent her a sign.

With a rare zeal, Daisy chopped the apples into slender slivers, and added raisins, rather wizened but still likely to have flavor, then spread it onto the rolled-out dough. As she added the remaining ingredients, she envisioned the pleasure that her siblings would have as they ate their piece of pie. It was true that the pieces would be small, but Mrs. Calloway would not begrudge the Stanley children their share. She too, enjoyed her sweets, although she didn't like to bake. Or cook, or clean, or mend, if the truth were known. Still, she was generous in her fashion and good to the little boys, who loved her in return.

Daisy worried about the amount of time Gus and Morris spent apart from their siblings. She, Gerald, Vera, and Eva were gone for most of the day, and they had little time to spend with their little brothers. She didn't know how to resolve the dilemma, especially since Mrs. Calloway displayed more maternal love to the boys than their own mother did. Daisy made certain that, each night, she told them a Bible story before they went to sleep, and she listened to their prayers. But it wasn't the same as the children of a family growing up together.

As she got older, Daisy had a more defined understanding of the kind of woman her mother had become. She refrained from criticizing her, but she could not help but feel betrayed by her mother. This was not what Papa would have wanted from his wife, even when he was no longer alive to be her husband.

Mrs. Calloway, lured by the aromas of the cooking food, appeared in the kitchen, having made a semblance of dressing for dinner by changing her frock and doing up her hair. "What's that I smell?" she asked, following her words with an exaggerated sniff. "It smells like apple pie!"

"It is apple pie," Daisy said, heartened by the landlady's appreciation. "I thought it was best to use up the apples before they turn. I made stew with the beef."

Mrs. Calloway nodded. "Bridey isn't to home," she said in an exaggerated whisper, "and said not to keep supper for her. So, there's more for us!" She quickly added, "Of course we'll put a plate aside for your ma, when she wakes."

Daisy simply nodded and began ladling stew into bowls. Katherine didn't seem to care much about eating. The last time Daisy had cleaned her mother's room, she'd found a half-empty bottle of whiskey underneath the bed. She had left it there, but she felt guilty knowing that it was the money from wages earned working at the textile mill that was funding Katherine's supply of liquor.

Daisy had said the blessing and they had all begun eating, their pleasure at the meal heightened by the knowledge that the pie in the center of the table awaited them when they'd finished their stew, when they heard the front door open. Mrs. Calloway muttered an oath. "Bridey told me she wouldn't be home," she said as she stood up. "And Big Jane is away looking after her sister who's just had her seventh."

Before Mrs. Calloway had even left the room, a man had come into the dining room. He had a smile on his face, but Daisy didn't think he looked friendly. When his eyes traveled around the table and rested upon Daisy, she didn't like the speculative gleam she saw.

"I'm here for my Katie," he said. "But if Katie is otherwise engaged, I certainly won't mind getting to know this pretty lass a wee bit better."

"This is Daisy," Mrs. Calloway said stiffly, outrage audible in her voice. "She's just twelve years old and she isn't planning on getting to know menfolk better any time soon."

"Daisy, eh?" the man said. "Flowers are for plucking. I reckon the time will come sooner than you think," he said, laughing at Mrs. Calloway. Then he turned and left the room. They heard his tread on the stairs. Then they heard the door to Katherine's room open.

"Don't pay him no never mind, children," Mrs. Calloway advised as she dipped her spoon into her bowl of stew. "We've got pie to look forward to and nothing can blight that."

But Daisy found that she had lost her appetite for pie.

GIRLS GROW UP FAST

Turning twelve had brought with it an assortment of complexities. It was not Katherine, but Mrs. Calloway, who had explained to Daisy that she wasn't a little girl anymore. Daisy had not felt like a little girl for ever so long, but she understood that Mrs. Calloway was referring to the changes in Daisy's appearance.

Daisy had noticed that, on the few times when she arrived home from the mill and Katherine had not left yet for the pub on the arm of whichever sailor was newly disembarked from his ship, she was getting attention of a sort that made her uncomfortable and made Katherine angry. The sailors—and they seemed to rotate, depending on whose ship was in port and which was out to sea—lingered at the front door of the boarding house as Daisy tried to enter. They engaged her in conversation, even though Katherine was at their side, and they looked at her in a way that made Daisy feel sullied.

Mrs. Calloway had noticed it too and, in her blunt, homespun way, was trying to help. "You're a fetching lass, Daisy, with that black hair and those dark eyes."

"I've always had black hair and dark eyes," Daisy said. She was tired and her feet were sore from the long day. She'd come home just after eight along with Gerald and her sisters, then made supper. Now she wanted to retreat to the room where her family was, to hear their prayers, and then go to bed herself. The morning, darker now with the onset of winter, came all too soon. "Gerald and me, we both take after Papa."

"It's not only the hair and eyes, although I'll grant you, they catch a man's eye. No, lass, it's what comes after that."

Daisy looked puzzled.

"You're growing into a young woman, Daisy. Your mother ought to be telling you things. Since she isn't, I warrant I'm the one meant to do it. The men . . . they've noticed. You know how to sew."

"Yes, of course,"

"Next pay, hold back some from what you give your ma. Buy yourself fabric and make a new dress. One that fits up top."

Daisy's skin turned red like the beets she'd served with supper. She was well aware that she was changing, Mrs. Calloway had given her a wooden screen for the bedroom so that the girls and boys were separated when they dressed and slept. At the time, Daisy had simply been grateful. Now she was embarrassed.

"Lass, it's the way of things. Natural. Girls grow into women and boys grow into men. But girls turn that corner faster than boys do. Now you make yourself a new dress. You can hand yours down to Vera, she'll be needing it soon, from the looks of things. And you do whatever you can to stay out of sight from your ma's gentlemen friends."

Daisy could not hide the fear in her eyes. "What—what do you mean?"

"Once a girl starts turning into a woman, some men don't bother to pay heed to whether she's twelve or twenty," Mrs. Calloway said cryptically. "It's best if they don't see you. Then they won't get confused, see?"

Daisy wasn't sure that she did see, but one thing was apparent. "Mrs. Calloway, if I keep back some of the money, there will be a frightful row with Mama. She knows what I bring her."

Mrs. Calloway sighed and patted Daisy on her hand. "Child, tell your ma that you lost an hour because you were late. Tell her you were disciplined for doing something you shouldn't have done. Tell her anything, but keep some of your own money."

"Those are falsehoods," Daisy protested. "The Bible says we're not to tell falsehoods."

Mrs. Calloway looked down at the tablecloth. The coals in the stove were still giving off heat, warding off the chill. The supper hadn't been much, just potatoes fried in onions and boiled beets, for money was tight now that cooler weather meant buying coal to stay warm, but the lingering odor of the cooking was a reminder that at least they'd all had a meal. The boarding house had been the Stanley family's home for six years and even though it was not the same as the miner's cottage where they had spent their early years while Papa was alive, this was home to them now. Daisy felt secure knowing that her brothers and sisters were upstairs, asleep and safe and fed.

She had taught the children the Ten Commandments. That was what Papa would have wanted. How could she break the rules of the Bible by telling a lie?

"Daisy, I know I don't go to church like I ought to. I do a lot of things I shouldn't. But I know this much. Sometimes in life, you have to choose between two sins, one the lesser and one the greater. Lying to your mother about holding back money for a dress isn't as great a sin as you might think."

"Lass," Mrs. Calloway said at last, "don't you reckon that God knows the difference between sins that can't be helped, and those that we help ourselves to?"

Daisy didn't understand what the plump landlady, with her hair an unlikely shade of gold and circles under her eyes from too many late nights, meant. It wasn't like Mrs. Calloway to talk about sin. Daisy wished there was someone she could talk to, someone who knew the Bible like Papa had known it. However, there was no one, and even if there had been, when would Daisy have the time to spend discussing the Bible? She had work to do during the week, cooking when she came home, and the children to mind.

She wondered, not with envy for that would be coveting, which the Bible forbade, what life was like for Annie Larkin, who still had both her parents to look after her and the other children. Daisy saw Annie in church on Sundays, and the pair exchanged rather shy smiles and greetings, but their circumstances had driven a chasm between them. Annie's mother would apprise her daughter of what growing up entailed and what to do when men bestowed unwelcome gazes upon her. Daisy had only the Bible as she understood it and the pragmatic, but well-meant advice of a landlady who frequented the nearby pub.

But Mrs. Calloway's instructions to avoid the men who escorted Katherine from the pub to her bedroom were not easy to follow over the years, and by the time Daisy was sixteen, even a new dress could not disguise the natural contours of her young woman's anatomy.

In the summer, dusk fell late. Daisy had taken on extra work when her shift at the textile mill ended. Her siblings, now with Gus and Morris joining Gerald, Vera, and Eva, went home at the usual time. Gerald and Vera replaced Daisy in cooking the evening meal for Mrs. Calloway's boarders. Daisy had found work as a seamstress' assistant. Her eyesight was good, and her needlework was excellent. It was a way to earn the extra money that was needed to make up for the pay that was lost each week so that the younger siblings could have one hour of schooling each week.

The seamstress for whom she worked, Mrs. Valentine, was an exacting mistress but not unreasonable in her expectations. Daisy worked until nine o'clock at night and then walked home. It was dark by then, and Daisy made her way from the mill to the boarding house by walking in the shadows of the buildings along the way. The streets which were familiar to her in the daylight took on a strange and sometimes sinister aspect. It seemed as if a nocturnal species occupied the nighttime streets. Alcohol was not always imbibed inside taverns and pubs. Men and women too staggered outside the drinking establishments, laughing and calling to one another. Sometimes they called out to Daisy, who hurried past. There were men and women engaged in carnal meetings, but they did not notice Daisy as she passed by.

It was with boundless relief that Daisy entered the boarding house. She opened the door with the key that Mrs. Calloway had given her to use and treaded quietly upon the stairs. She was weary, her shoulders slumped and her eyelids drooping, as she laboriously ascended each step.

As she stepped onto the landing, the door of her mother's room opened, revealing for a scant moment the long, narrow angle of light before it closed again.

Daisy looked up, startled. She sensed a presence, and there was movement, but the darkness of the staircase was too opaque to allow her to discern details.

"Pretty li'l thing." A low, rough voice, its speaker concealed by the absence of light, broke the silence. Daisy knew she had heard the voice before, but she couldn't remember from where.

Daisy backed against the wooden railing. The voice continued to speak from the shadows.

"I said that one day, the time would come," the voice went on, amused, assured, and a little drunk. Daisy had lived at the boarding house long enough to tell when someone was the worse for drink. Usually, when Katherine had had what Mrs. Calloway described as "one too many," her words were slurred when she spoke, and she moved with an awkward gait. Daisy could not tell how this man's movements were affected, as he remained cloaked in the staircase shadows; his voice was thickened with liquor's remnants, but she could tell by his voice that he was smiling—

Smiling! This was the man who'd interrupted their supper years ago, the man who had leered at her as she sat with Mrs. Calloway and her siblings at the table. This man was the reason Mrs. Calloway had given her the warning about men who didn't care if a girl was of a proper age to receive attention from a gentleman. This man, of course, was no gentleman.

"Go on home," Daisy said with a firmness she was far from feeling. She knew that at this hour, Mrs. Calloway and the other female boarders would be at the pub. It was too early, although it was nighttime, for them to be at home. Katherine was probably still asleep after providing the companionship for this sailor that Daisy now knew was more than pleasant conversation. "You've no business here!"

"Oh, but I have," the man said in a mocking tone. "You're my business, pretty l'il girl. I have a fancy to see you now that you're old enough to wear your hair down. Or do you still have those black braids?"

She heard the stair creak. Daisy shrank back, the wood railing hard against her waist. She couldn't stay where she was, but she didn't dare move.

Another stair made a sound as the man stepped upon it. Daisy felt as if her very breath must be frozen inside her chest. She had to get away.

Desperate by now, Daisy tried to rush up the stairs. The man lunged forward. His arm brushed hers. Daisy cried out as he grabbed her by the wrist. She jerked backwards to free herself from his grasp. As she did so, the door to Katherine's room opened.

The light from the lamp in her room illuminated the stairs. "What are you doing?" Katherine demanded of Daisy. "How dare you—"

Daisy wrested herself free from the sailor's grasp and ran past him. The sailor lost his footing and tumbled to the foot of the stairs, where he lay still and crumpled on the floor.

"You've killed him!" Katherine yelled out. "You'll hang for this!"

Katherine, holding onto the railing, made her way down the stairs. "My darling," she crooned in a drunken, singsong voice as she cradled the sailor's head in her arms. "She'll pay for what she's done, I prom—I promise you!"

Daisy ran into the bedroom where her brothers and sisters, now awakened by the noise, sat up in their beds, staring at their sister in bewildered fear.

"We have to leave," Daisy told them, her actions matching her words as she went to the battered wooden trunk where their clothing was stored. "As soon as we can get away, we must go!"

BACK TO THE MINE

They didn't dare take the stairs to make their escape; they could hear Katherine's drunken keening and moaning as she wailed for her lost love and berated her daughter for murdering her true love. Daisy was caught in a quandary: if she had truly caused the sailor to lose his life, albeit unintentionally, then she was indeed a criminal who deserved to face justice, however unfair.

It was Vera, now fourteen, who quelled her older sister's conscience. "If he's dead, it's his own miserable fault. You know what he was after. If he hadn't fallen down the stairs, he'd have attacked you and then where would you be? You'd have to get the law on him, and who's to say they'd even bother to come? It's for us to get away and find a place where all of us will be safe. And where you won't be bothered by the likes of Mama's wretched lovers!"

To hear such damning words from her younger sister, who with her lustrous blonde hair and curving figure was the very image of their mother a decade ago, was startling. But Gerald, now fifteen with the imprint of his father's countenance in his features, waiting only for manhood to make him Wilbur Stanley's twin, nodded solemnly.

"Vera is right," he said to Daisy as Vera turned her attention to helping the younger boys pack up their meager belongings in their knapsacks, "we're best out of here. There's no telling what Mama might do or say when the drink wears off."

"I wish—" But Daisy didn't finish. She didn't know what to wish. She could wish that the mine hadn't collapsed ten years ago. But what good would wishing do now? Papa had been dead ten years and if they didn't get away from their mother and the boarding house and the sailor that Daisy had murdered, Daisy would hang, and her brothers and sisters would go to the orphanage or the poorhouse.

Daisy nodded. "Mrs. Calloway and the others won't be back for a few hours yet. Mama—" her voice choked on the word that conjured memories of what Katherine had once been to them, and how far their mother had fallen from those maternal days. Steeling herself, Daisy continued. "Mama may not come back upstairs for hours yet either. She—she'll have to summon the constable, but she's—"

"Mama is too drunk to think clearly," Vera said impatiently. "She's not thinking of us, she's thinking of him if she has any thoughts in her head at all. We're ready to go. We can climb out the window from the bedroom. The roof is low. We don't have far to drop. I want to get away from here before—" Vera's lip trembled. "I don't want anyone to hurt you, Daisy. You've been more of a mother to us than Mama. We can't lose you!"

Daisy, always the sister who looked after the others, was touched by Vera's display of concern. The others were nodding their heads in agreement. They were all ready to go; Gerald had shepherded the boys into their caps and coats while Vera had done the same for the girls. Each one bore a knapsack.

The trunk was nearly empty now. The belongings they had carried with them in the pushcart from their old home near the mine to their lodgings in the boarding house had long since been sold over the years to pay for necessities when their earnings weren't enough. But there were a few things left.

"Each of us must take one of the toys that Papa carved," Daisy said. "It's all we have of him."

Eva began to object. "We've already packed, Daisy—"

But Gerald interceded. "The toys aren't big," he said. "They'll fit inside our clothing."

Daisy nodded, grateful to her brother for his support. The children did as they were bade, and then they stood patiently. Waiting.

"Gerald, you go down first," Daisy said as she opened the window. The nighttime air was cool, but not cold. They would be all right, at least for now, while the summer weather accommodated their circumstances. What they would do when cold weather came was more than Daisy could fathom.

Gerald was backing out of the window. His dark hair and clothing blended into the night. Then he was out of sight, but they heard the soft thump as he reached the ground.

The girls went next, followed by the boys, in the order of their birth. Daisy looked out the window at the five upturned heads waiting for her to join them.

She looked around the room for one last time. It had been the place where they had lived for the last ten years. But it had never really been home.

She tossed her knapsack out the window, then carefully stepped out, holding her skirts aside so that she didn't get tangled up in the cloth. The thick grass behind the boarding house cushioned her drop to the ground.

Daisy looked up at the sky. There was a half moon to see by, and stars to help them along their way. God was providing for them. Even if she had sinned and done murder, God was not abandoning her.

"Where are we going?" Morris, now eleven years old, asked plaintively. He knew no home but the boarding house and as irregular as his upbringing had been, it was familiar to him.

Daisy gave him a comforting hug. "We'll walk to Oldham," she said as if she had given the matter consideration, although in truth, the solution had just come to her. "We'll go down into one of the abandoned mines and stay there until we have come up with a plan."

Eva, thirteen, whimpered. "Not the mines, Daisy," she begged. "Not where Papa died."

Daisy, with one arm around Morris and the other around Eva, hugged them fiercely. "The abandoned mines are ones where the veins of coal played out," she explained, the miners' ways coming back to her readily. "The men stopped going down there because there was no more coal. We'll be safe there. No one will think to find us there and we'll have a place to hide."

Gerald nodded in approval and gave his sister one of his rare smiles. "Right good thinking, Daisy," he said.

The Stanley children set off on the familiar route. They knew all the pathways and back routes that would take them to Oldham without exposing them to any nocturnal traffic or passersby. They also knew where the orchards and gardens were, and each one took the time, as they walked, to pick an apple from the tree, or pluck carrots or green peppers from the earth. Daisy, who had never allowed them to filch the fruit or vegetables before as they walked to and from church, did not dissuade them now.

She wondered if she ought to do so. But then she remembered Mrs. Calloway's assurance. *"Sometimes in life, you have to choose between two sins, one the lesser and one the greater."*

This was such a time. Stealing was a sin; violating it was a violation of the commandments that God had given to Moses. But if the children did not have food, they would starve and die. She still had to take care of them. She would not let them starve. God would understand.

The children had worked at the mill during the day as usual, and they had not had much sleep before the drunken sailor had fallen down the stairs. They were tired, and frightened. As hard as their lives had been before, there was a certainty to their routine. They would go to work and earn their pay and go home to the boarding house to eat and sleep. Now they were unsure of where they would live; an abandoned mine could not provide a home. They had no certainty that there would be food for them except for what they could forage, and that was by no means a safe or guaranteed source of nourishment. They could all end up before the constable on charges of thievery, for the local farmers were not so kind of heart to be solicitous of hungry children making off with the produce the working men harvested for their own livelihoods. But there was nothing to be done but continue walking. Their only hope rested in finding the abandoned mine that Daisy sought so that they could take their rest.

Although the children returned to Oldham each Sunday for church services, it was Daisy who had the best recollection of the town where she had lived until she turned six years old. Papa had told her all about the mines; he had grown up in Oldham and she remembered his stories as if he were still alive to tell them.

They were approaching an area which was overgrown with weeds. The ramshackle cottages had caved-in roofs, decrepit walls, some of which had fallen to the ground, and windows which had long since lost their panes of glass. Although it was dark, the half moon provided them with the light Daisy needed to distinguish the trail, overgrown now with disuse, that led to the abandoned mine. The opening to the mine was concealed with thick weeds. Gerald came forward, his pocketknife in hand.

"I'll cut them away," he said quietly, "so we can go in. Then we'll pull the clumps of weeds back over the opening, from the inside, so that no one can tell it's been disturbed."

Daisy nodded. She doubted if anyone came this way anymore now that the mine was not used, but Gerald was wise to suggest caution. He led the way down the mine, the children following with trepidation, for the mine was dark and the access was narrow. When they were out of the entry tunnel and in an open area, their eyes needed to adjust to the absence of light that made the mine even darker than the night outside.

It was cool inside the mine, but the air seemed fresh. Daisy knew how important that was because Papa had told her that sometimes, the air in a mine could be poisonous. She wished they could see their surroundings, but that would have to wait until daylight. Perhaps then they would be able to have a better grasp of the abandoned mine; perhaps a miner had left a tool there, or a canteen. It was not likely, but it was possible.

"We'd best try to sleep now," she said, forcing herself to speak with a confident air even though she, too, felt fear.

Gerald had managed the children well. Each one had folded up bedding to pack inside the knapsack. It was their own bedding from their mining cottage home, and nothing stolen from Mrs. Calloway. Daisy had been firm on that score. The landlady had been kind to them, and they would not rob her of what was hers.

"It's best if we don't make noise," she whispered. "We don't want any stragglers wandering by to hear us and decide they want to investigate why voices are coming from an abandoned mine. But each of you, think your prayers tonight rather than say them. God has found us a place of safety and we must not be ungrateful to Him for his care."

Using their knapsacks for pillows, the children wrapped their blankets around them and huddled together for warmth. Daisy listened to the sounds of their breathing and was able to tell when each one fell asleep. Only when the last one awake, Eva, had finally surrendered to slumber could Daisy close her eyes.

But before she did, she too had to think her prayers.

"Precious Father," she said, beginning her prayers as Papa had taught her and she had continued in teaching the younger ones, "Thou hast brought us out of the wilderness to safety, just as Thou didst for the Children of Israel. We offer you thanks that Thou hast found refuge for us. Forgive me, Lord God, for killing the sailor. Thou knowest that was not my intention. I am innocent. I pray for his soul, nonetheless. I pray for my brothers and sisters. Thou art the only hope we have, the only source of strength and comfort. We will need food and water, and we will need a place to live, for we cannot stay here past the summer. Keep us in Thy care, I pray, and bring us to the Promised Land. Amen."

Daisy did not know where the Promised Land might be. It would be enough if she could find a place where they could all stay together in safety, with enough to eat, to be able to sleep securely and to avoid attention from the law. She did not want to be hanged. She had not meant for the sailor to die. But more than her own possible death by hanging if she were apprehended, Daisy feared for the wellbeing of her brothers and sisters. Papa had always taught her that the most important charge for anyone was to obey God and look after one's family.

At sixteen years of age, Daisy could honestly attest that she had committed herself to doing both those things.

THE LESSER SIN

How had Papa endured it? Daisy wondered. Being down in the mine, which had been Papa's means of making a living, felt as if she were in a tomb. It was a refuge for the Stanley children, but at what a cost! Even though Papa had left the mine each day and returned home to the cottage to be with his family, he had to go back, day after day, so that he could feed his family and house them. But all that time, he had known that death in the mine was a possibility.

Her fate was a different one. Their first priority was to find food. That meant stealing it, for they had no means to buy what they needed. They were in hiding to elude the law because Daisy was at risk. There was no way for them to find out whether the legal authorities were on the hunt for Daisy or not. They dared not be seen in public, for the Stanleys were familiar faces to the Oldham community. While Daisy did not think that Mrs. Larkin would have turned her into the constable, how could she be sure? A charge of murder was no minor offense. It was a hanging offense.

Daisy, in turmoil by the desperation of their situation and her sense of guilt that she was the cause of it, did not know what to do. Mrs. Calloway's words came back to her. *"Sometimes in life, you have to choose between two sins, one the lesser and one the greater."*

They had to eat. Even if they had money, which they did not, they could not have gone to the shops or market to buy food. That meant stealing it. After a night spent in restless sleep, Daisy awoke early the next morning, although she had no way of knowing for sure what time it was. She rose from the makeshift bed and gently tapped Gerald on his shoulder. The speed with which he responded told her that he had not had a restful night either.

He followed his sister out of the mine chamber and back up in the tunnel where they could speak and not awaken their sisters and brothers. Daisy was also aware that they had to keep their voices low so that they would not be overheard if someone above ground was making his way home through the area around the mine. The abandonment of the mine had seen the cottages around the mine fall into disrepair as well, and it was unlikely that anyone would be aware of the Stanley children's abode. Still, they could not take any chances.

Gerald listened attentively as Daisy outlined their situation. His young face, sober beyond his youth, revealed no surprise when his sister told him what they had to do. She realized, with dismay, that Gerald had accepted the nuances of their circumstances more realistically than she had.

"I'll take my knapsack," he said quietly, his voice so soft that his whisper was almost as light as a breath of air. "The gardens are ripe. So are the orchards. There might be an egg or two in the chicken coops that haven't been gathered."

"I don't know how we'll cook eggs," Daisy said, biting her lip as she considered this other quandary.

"First to get the eggs," Gerald advised with a smile all the more remarkable because he was not one for mirth, "then we'll fuss about cooking them."

"You and I will let the others know what we're doing," Daisy said. "We'll go at night when we're less likely to be seen."

"It'll mean a hungry day," Gerald warned. As hard as things had been working long days at the mill, the children had had supper at the boarding house, and they'd had bread for their lunches. "I can go out now, while it's early and see what I might find."

"No! It's too dangerous!" Daisy argued. "I won't have you taking such a chance because of me."

"This isn't your fault, Daisy," Gerald disputed.

"It is my fault," Daisy fretted. "I should have done something—"

"Done what?" her brother asked. "Let him attack you? You know what he intended. It's for Mama to protect you and she didn't. You were protecting us, just as you've always done since Papa died. Now we're with you because we want to be. We'll come right through this, Daisy. Doesn't the Bible tell us that God will not abandon us no matter how hard our trials?"

Daisy bit her lip. How strange it was to hear her younger brother offering the same words of comfort that she had used throughout their childhood when her siblings needed reassurance. "Yes," she acknowledged. "But not in the daylight, please Gerald. I'd never forgive myself if you were caught. And what would we do if you were? We'd have no way of knowing what happened. No, we'll go at night, together. Vera has a steady head on her shoulders. She'll be here with Eva, Gus and Morris. She'll look after them."

So began their nocturnal routine. When the sun had long since set in the sky and darkness had spread its broad cloak over their secluded hideaway, Daisy and Gerald crept out of the mine. They reassembled the cluster of weeds that Gerald had cut away so that they could enter the mine, using the brambles as a most unusually hinged door.

The night was cloudy, but perhaps the absence of illumination would work in their favor, Daisy thought, determined to put the most promising setting to their plight. She turned back to make sure that the mine gave away nothing of its secrets.

"No one can tell," Gerald said, noticing her action and deciphering her thoughts. "I doubt anyone comes 'round this way anyway. It looks as if it hasn't seen a human being but us in a long time."

Daisy knew that an abandoned mine was soon forgotten. Where there was no coal to be dug, there was no money to be made. Mine owners sent their workers elsewhere to find more profitable mines in which to labor. Before long, the community which had housed families became desolate. Folks avoided the area, uneasy in the presence of such desolation. Stories began to spread, claiming that the mine was haunted.

Those stories would help to keep them safe, Daisy knew. There was nothing haunted about the abandoned mine except for the dead hopes and live fears that flourished. Daisy wondered if, perhaps, that was worse than the ghosts of the dead.

∼

It didn't seem right to take food from the gardens of the miners who barely had enough to live on themselves, as Daisy knew full well. But that first night, creeping along the shadow side of cabins and houses that seemed unfamiliar to them without sunlight overhead, Daisy was too frightened to venture far. She vowed silently to God, as she pulled carrots from the Larkin garden, that she would pay back everything one day. Down to the last carrot.

The next night, she and Gerald knew that they needed to venture farther from the community to forage for food. She refused to call it stealing, even though she knew that she was violating the eighth commandment, which clearly said "Thou shalt not steal." She could only cling to the hope that God would hold her to the same understanding of His will that Mrs. Calloway had told her, and that stealing food for her family was a lesser violation than letting them go hungry.

The others were grateful for the vegetables, certainly, and no one complained. But Daisy and Gerald understood that vegetables were not the same as oatmeal or potato soup or a meat pie. With that tacit understanding in mind, the two eldest of the Stanley children decided to make their way beyond the boundaries of Oldham and head toward Ebbot's Acre, a village to the south where they weren't known. But they had to leave while the shops were still open, which was when the vendors were out selling their foods.

She and Gerald washed their faces in the brook that was not far from the abandoned mine. It was near a section of rundown miners' cabins and across from a field of wild daisies. Amidst so much that was so badly in need of repair and well past the point of being livable, the daisies were a reminder that beauty had not left the town.

Daisy felt a tiny glimmer of optimism as they passed the daisies. She saw Gerald look over at her, as if to make sure that she had noticed them. She gave her brother a smile and nodded. Daisies weren't food or shelter, but God had put them in the earth to grow for a purpose.

As they left Oldham behind and drew nearer to Ebbot's Acre, Daisy and Gerald were at first perturbed to see that, although dusk was falling, people were milling about as if it were earlier. But as they entered the town, they realized why. There was a fair! Where there was a fair, there was food.

"We'll need to be very careful," Daisy whispered to her brother as they approached the row of stalls, the aromas of food tantalizingly close. "If we're noticed, we'll have no way of getting away with so many people about."

Gerald nodded. "One item from each stall," he said.

That was sensible. Daisy wished they had a means of providing a distraction, but they did not and would have to rely on the crowds to conceal them, and God to assist them. it hardly seemed proper to ask God for help in their thievery, but the Stanley children had no one but God to care about them.

They instinctively followed the scents of the food wafting around them. The emptiness of their hunger left plenty of room for the aromas to find lodgings inside their nostrils: meat seasoned with onions frying over a flame; the succulent scent of ham from another direction; toasted bread sending its homing scent out to all who passed by; fruit pies made with berries, or apples, or luscious plums . . . every stall was a feasting table to the two Stanleys who had eaten nothing but stolen vegetables the day before.

Gerald inhaled deeply as if by doing so, he would somehow feel nourished by the food. "I'd settle for a good wedge of bread," he said reverently, "with a piece of cheese, and a hot cup of tea," he told his sister, "and account myself a king."

Daisy heard him, but her eyes were alert for opportunity and then she saw it. The man running the meat pie stall was assisted by a youngster, likely his son, who was rather slapdash in putting the baked pies out to sell. As one was sold, he pushed the others further down the wooden plank that served as a countertop. Daisy waited for the right moment, and it soon arrived. A man and a woman, perhaps a married couple, bought five meat pies, no doubt for the children running about in front of the stall. The young boy put new pies down to replace those that had been sold, pushed without looking, and one fell off the end of the plank.

The boy didn't notice. He was listening to his father, who was occupied in putting crust on another batch before heating them over the flame. Daisy darted down to the ground, scooped up the fallen pie, and had put it in her knapsack before anyone noticed.

Gerald nodded his approval. That was how it was done, and now he knew what to do. The Stanleys would eat well as long as the fair was in town. It was thieving as surely as the Stanleys were runaways, but Daisy was right with God and Gerald trusted that the Lord would understand that it was either steal or starve. As he had heard Daisy say more than once, the Stanleys had only God to defend them now.

UNWANTED

"A man of twenty ought to be on his own," Priscilla Dalton complained as she set out plates for the evening meal. "Not loitering at home, living off his father."

"If by loitering you mean milking the cows, slopping the pigs, mucking out the stable, plowing the fields, and feeding the chickens, I'm eager to learn what you think a full day's work entails," Perry, his voice raised, demanded. "You'll not learn of it from Albert, I can tell you that. It's a marvel that he hasn't got splinters in his backside from sitting all day."

Priscilla slammed the pot of stew down on the table. Albert Eddings protested as hot drops of the broth fell upon his hand.

"Ma, you'll burn me with your carelessness," he shouted at his mother.

"Albert has a bad heart, he was born with it," Priscilla said to Perry, her pale blue eyes almost as white as ice as she glared at her stepson. "He can't be doing farm labor. That's why I sent him to school, so he can earn a living while he works inside."

"He's doing precious little of that," Perry retorted. "If he's not sitting by the fire, he's down at the tavern."

"I'm going to be setting up business for myself," Albert defended himself. "Those men will be my clients when I'm doing bookkeeping. In the meantime, I'm tending to the accounts for the farm, and that, for your information, is what I'm doing when I'm home during the day."

"It doesn't take a solid day's effort to tally up the amount that's paid for hay, and seeds, and—"

"You know nothing of accounting," Albert said with a superior sniff as he moved his elbows so that his mother could set the bowl of stew before him.

"I know that figures in a column don't take all day to add up," Perry said.

"Boys," Samuel Dalton intervened with a weak wave of his hand. "I won't have this fighting at the table. It's disrespectful to your mother."

Perry forbore from making the point that Priscilla Eddings Dalton, the widow that Sam Dalton had wed four years ago, was not his mother. She was a domineering, foul-tempered woman who bullied her second husband, doted on the son she'd borne to her late husband, and harassed Perry whenever they had the misfortune to be in proximity.

He muttered his thanks when Priscilla put his bowl of stew in front of him. He was not surprised to see that his portion was mostly potatoes, peas, carrots, and broth, with almost no chunks of beef in the mix. Albert would have gotten the bulk of the meat, and Pa would have gotten second best. Priscilla would fill her bowl to her own satisfaction and Perry would have to be satisfied with what was left.

Perry paid no attention to the conversation at the table. Priscilla was complaining about the vicar's wife, who, she claimed, was putting on airs by donning a new bonnet. Albert was making his case that a conveyance more impressive than the sturdy old wooden wagon was needed for his travels.

"How can I hope to entice business when I don't even have a proper carriage, not to mention my own horse," he grumbled.

It never seemed to bother the pair that their conversations were never in tandem, or that they spoke at one another, intent upon their personal topics. Somehow, though, they seemed to communicate, for Priscilla seized upon her son's lament.

"I'm sure there's money to spare from the earnings we get when we sell in the market," she said to her husband, lubricating her words with an oily, insinuating tone. "Albert will find the money, won't you, dear?"

"Why do we need more than one horse?" Sam Dalton, at last prodded into a response, spoke up. "Lacey does all that we need."

"Lacey," Albert explained as if he were speaking to a dim child, "is a farm horse. As an aspiring man of business, I need a horse with some flash to him. Something to attest to my professional attributes."

Although Perry tried to be oblivious to his stepbrother's ludicrous claims, the absurdity of this assertion goaded him into a response.

"I've seen the other 'men of business' about the town," he said. "I see them in their offices, their shops, when I'm going to market. I see them, Albert. They aren't lolling at home doing nothing but predicting how fashionable they'll be when they've established themselves."

"A lot you know about fashion!" Priscilla yelled. "You in your work trousers and your cotton shirt and your boots, you've got farmhand written all over you."

"Not 'farmhand,' Priscilla," Perry said, leaning across the table, his blue eyes steely and his jaw set like it had been cast in iron. "Farmer's son. Farmer's son, and heir, Priscilla," he continued. "Son and heir. This farm has been in the Dalton family for generations. The Daltons were farming this land when the Eddings were hiring themselves out to help with the spring planting."

His stepmother didn't appreciate being reminded of her late husband's humble beginnings, mostly because she felt they reflected poorly on her son's chances of a better life. "Mind your tongue, you insolent boy," she seethed. "Folks who fall upon hard times do as they can. You might find yourself in the same fix one day."

"And so I might," Perry returned. "But what will you do then? Will Albert and that convenient bad heart of his work the land with Pa while I hire out? I'd pay good money to see Albert at the plow, that I would."

"This farm ought to go to my son," Priscilla shouted. Her plump cheeks were mottled with the red flushes of rage. "He's smarter than you'll ever be. He can make something of himself which is more than you'll ever do."

"This farm, and the work that Pa and I do, puts food on the table," Perry shouted back, his ire at his stepmother overflowing from his efforts to control his temper.

"Perry," Pa chided. "That's no way to speak to your stepmother."

Father and son locked gazes. They were alike in looks, in build, even in their voices, but Perry felt that his father had surrendered his manhood to the virago of a woman he'd married after Perry's mother had died of tuberculosis five years ago. Anne Dalton had been gentle and kind, devoted to her husband and her son, with never a malicious word for anyone. How, with that example so fresh in his mind, had Pa taken leave of his senses and married Priscilla Eddings? Perry didn't understand it, but he had vowed that when he was seeking a wife, he'd make certain that he found a woman who was loyal and true, willing to share in good times and bad.

"Pa," Perry said urgently, striving to penetrate that unfathomable wall behind which his father seemed to take refuge when the subject of the farm and its ownership rose. "This farm has been worked by Daltons since there were Stuarts on the throne of England." He looked up at the smoke-blackened beams of the kitchen that testified to the generations of ancestors who had sat here around the table and eaten their meals. He pointed with his knife at the window; outside the glass panes, the lush green fields of the Dalton farm were a constant reminder of the work that had gone into maintaining this land. "Are you going to throw it away for a lazy sluggard who'll never stand to a day's work?"

"Who are you calling a sluggard?" Albert wanted to know, his face taking on the same red-and-white coloring as his mother when rage painted his skin.

"You, obviously," Perry said, too angry to restrain himself.

Sam Dalton slammed his big fist upon the table. "I'm the master of this household," he called out, "and I'll have none of this talk from you. Do I make myself clear?"

If Pa had included Albert in his scolding, the course of Perry's life might have run very differently. But it was too much, both for the young man's pride and for his affection for his father, to endure. He stood up from his chair.

He was a tall young man, so tall that he needed to duck from the low beams that had been built to accommodate men of lesser height. He was broad-shouldered like his father, and like past Daltons, he had vivid blue eyes that brought to mind the skies of a fertile summer and the fair hair that evoked the color of the hay in the loft. But Perry was about to do something that his Dalton forbears had not thought of doing.

"If that's the way it's to be," he said, his voice throbbing with emotion, "then this isn't a place I can call home any longer."

"Perry," his father rose as well, meeting his son's eyes with his own blue gaze. "I must have peace under my roof."

"Your peace, and your roof, aren't deserving of my surrender, Pa. I'm your son and I've treated you as a faithful son. You've made your choice."

He pushed his chair in and went up the narrow flight of stairs, closing his memory to the thoughts of how often, as a boy, he'd bounded down each stair in his eagerness to follow his father out to the farm. Perry opened the door to his bedroom. It didn't take long to pack his belongings.

He bent down and found the loose floorboard under the bed where he kept the coins that he'd saved over the years, the profits from the eggs he had sold in the market. It was money that his mother and father had allowed him to keep for his own, for the farm was profitable enough with the yield of the garden, the meat that was slaughtered, and the milk that the dairy cows produced. The chickens had been Perry's to tend and care for. That work, and his savings, would give him some money to start his new life.

There was one more thing to bring. He took the small wooden box out and opened it. It was his mother's wedding ring, given to her by his father on the day they were wed. After she died, Pa had taken it from her finger. "It's yours now, son," he'd said, his voice choked with sobs he was holding back. "Someday you'll find a wife and I pray you'll have as much happiness with her as I've had with your mother."

Perry packed the box away with his other belongings. Someday, he'd find that wife. But now, he had to find his own way in the world.

Perry stood for a long, labored moment, scanning the plain walls that had witnessed his risings and his sleeping for over twenty years. He realized with a pang that his entire life had been played out upon the stage of this room, and the kitchen downstairs where the family had shared their meals, the sitting room where they had retired after the day's work was done. Happy times, mostly, until his mother's illness forced Perry and his father to prepare themselves for her unavoidable death. Even the sad times now were precious, because Perry knew that, in leaving this house, he was leaving his childhood behind.

He walked down the stairs with a slow gait. He was not in haste to leave. He would not return here. He knew that.

When he entered the kitchen, he saw that Priscilla and Albert were still eating, having resumed their disjointed conversation as if there had been no disruption. His father sat immobile in his chair, his stew untouched. Perry could not leave his father without some acknowledgment of the past joys.

"Pa," he said, standing beside Sam Dalton, "it's time for me to go. But I'll take the memories of the happy times with you and Ma with me."

Priscilla started to speak but Sam held up his hand to halt her. "I'm talking to my son," he said.

He put his hand on Perry's shoulder. "I didn't want this," he said.

Was there a tear in Sam Dalton's blue eyes? Perry thought he saw a glistening there. He bit his lip to prevent his own threatening tears to fall.

"You've been a good son, Perry," Pa said. "You've been a credit to the Daltons. I couldn't ask for more from a son."

He held out his hand. Perry took it and the two men, joined by lineage and memories, put the words they could not express into their grip.

"Go with God, Perry," Pa said.

∼

It wasn't easy for Perry to adjust to working underground in the dark, gloomy coal mine when he'd been accustomed to spending his days with the sun on his back. For a farmer, the weather was a constant factor far beyond comfort. The sun, rain, and wind were partners in the harvest. Now, instead of scanning the skies overhead to decide how his day would go, Perry sometimes didn't see the sun at all. He went to the mine before the sun had risen, and he left its confines when dusk was already falling.

He got along well enough with the other miners, but he was a newcomer to Oldham and the miners were used to their own community. When his shift was done, Perry walked back to his cottage. His meals consisted of whatever he could catch—a rabbit running through the overgrowth, or a fish from the nearby brook—and the vegetables that he bought in the market when he had a chance to go into town on his days off from work. But the cost of items in the company-owned store was prohibitive and Perry spent sparingly, buying only what he could not do without. It was a rough-hewn sort of life, but it was better than the daily conflict with his stepmother.

There were no cottages to be had; they went to families. But he managed to find lodgings, of a sort, in a rundown cottage located near an abandoned mine that had ceased to be profitable for the owners a decade ago. It was in great need of repair, and Perry had no tools to do the work, but he managed as best he could, patching the holes in the roof with thatch from the overgrowth of vegetation that surrounded the little house.

The open windows were no travail in the warmth of summer, but he didn't know how he'd manage in the cold of winter. Occasionally, a bird flew in through the gaping window and would perch upon the sill, studying him with a curious glance as if wondering why he was there.

Perry welcomed such diversions, for he found that the loneliness was worse than the discomfort. At least the summer, with its constant evidence of life in the animals that scampered across the ground and in the air, and the green leaves bursting from the branches that would be bare in winter, gave him hope. But he wondered how he would manage when the isolation of winter closed in upon him.

PERIL AT THE MARKET PLACE

Daisy was not at peace with the fact that, if she and Gerald didn't steal, her family would have nothing to eat. The truth was that she and Gerald had become adept at thieving from the stalls on market day. Vera managed as best she could, staying inside the abandoned mine and turning their shelter into a home. They took turns venturing from the mine, adhering to Daisy's instructions to remain out of sight. They brought water from the brook for drinking, and Vera, having found a battered old basin deeper in the mine, scrubbed it as clean as she could make it so that they could wash. Daisy didn't like the thoughts of her sisters and brothers exploring deeper in the mines, but she could not deny their success. The mine had been abandoned, it was true, but the miners had left behind items that proved useful to the Stanley children: a bucket that could be used for carrying water; rags that, when washed and dried, were perfectly good as towels and facecloths; plates from a forgotten meal; even candles and matches that, lighted sparingly, provided some relief from the darkness inside the mine.

Sometimes Morris and Gus spoke longingly of the boarding house, the only home they remembered, and the sweets that Mrs. Calloway always had on hand. But they only talked about these things when Daisy and Gerald were not with them, for their older siblings had different memories of another time when they had been a family and lived in a cottage, and Mama cooked meals and didn't come home from the tavern with men. Vera remembered those times as well, but she was old enough now to realize how much responsibility had been placed upon Daisy and Gerald because of the way that Mama had changed after Papa's death. She remembered, but she kept her silence when the younger ones were nostalgic for their beds and their hot suppers and all that they had left behind. Vera knew that Mama had failed to protect Daisy from the unwanted attentions of one of Mama's lovers. She could not be a loyal daughter and sister both, and so she had chosen to give her loyalty to Daisy.

Daisy and Gerald set off for the village on market day, as they did every week. Daisy was concerned that they would attract attention; they were strangers to the village where they stole food, and she worried that someone would notice that they were without parents.

Gerald didn't agree. "We're not little children," he pointed out. "You're sixteen, I'm fifteen but I look older than you. You're old enough to be a wife. No one will notice."

It seemed odd to Daisy to think that many girls her age were already mothers. Katherine had been married at sixteen years. Daisy knew that she was a woman in her body. The sailor who had tried to grope her on the staircase at Mrs. Calloway's boarding house had been proof of her maturity. She didn't like to think about that.

"They might notice that we come to the market every week, but we never buy anything," Daisy noted. "Yet our sacks are always filled."

"We have only to be careful, Daisy," Gerald said. "What other choice do we have? We can't let the others starve."

He and Daisy had already talked about what they would need to do before summer ended and fall came with its colder weather. When winter came, and the gardens were barren, the market day would be lean and there would be few opportunities to obtain food. Daisy thought of their plight constantly, even though the days were still warm. She knew, as did Gerald, that living in an abandoned mine, while it offered shelter of a sort, was hardly a home. The mine was dark; whenever any of the Stanley children ventured outside in the morning, their entrance into the sunlit day left them blinking until their eyes adjusted to the light. For Daisy and Gerald, who spent more of each day outside finding food, there was respite from their underground living, but the younger members of the family could only emerge outside furtively, less they be noticed by anyone who would know who they were and call the constable.

Thus far, they had been lucky in avoiding notice. They were all fearful that Daisy would be captured, imprisoned, and hanged for her role in the death of their mother's sailor lover. That was reason enough to keep the younger Stanleys willingly concealed as much as possible.

But it was not a good life, and Daisy felt guilty that she should be the cause of it. What would they do when the cold weather came? Upon occasion, she and Gerald would surreptitiously steal clothes that were drying outside on a line when women had done laundry. A shirt here, a pair of stockings there, slowly and painstakingly acquired so that the children could supplement the meager wardrobes they'd brought with them when they'd fled the boarding house. Clothing was one thing, but how could they steal blankets to keep warm at night? And fuel would be impossible.

Daisy tried not to let these worries occupy her mind, especially when she knew she had to keep her wits about her. Stealing, she had learned, was not easy. It required alertness and dexterity. It was necessary to watch not only the shopkeeper or vendor so that his goods were pilfered when his back was turned, but also an awareness of the others in the vicinity who would raise the alarm if they saw theft taking place. She and Gerald worked together in order to avoid attracting attention as much as possible.

The marketplace was thronged with people. That was good. The day was warm, and people were in a jolly mood as they surveyed the goods displayed in the stalls where the vendors sold their wares. Lettuces, beans, and radishes were displayed invitingly upon the counters, but Daisy didn't linger over these, as much as she longed for fresh vegetables. She was looking for items which could be eaten easily with their insufficient cutlery and dishware. That meant pieces of cooked meat, or individual pieces of fruit such as apples or pears, hunks of cheese . . . or bread.

The baker, a dour-visaged man who, because he knew that everyone needed bread, saw no reason to be gracious to his customers, put his loaves of bread out for sale and stood behind them, his arms folded across his chest, glowering at customers. When one loaf was sold, he replaced it with another, but his countenance never brightened, even though he seemed to be doing a brisk business.

Bread would fill their bellies, even if there was nothing else to go with it. It was easy to stuff into the knapsack, light to carry, and not an impediment if they needed to leave the marketplace quickly.

Daisy gave a subtle nod to Gerald, the signal for him to keep watch on the other people around the stall while Daisy focused her attention on the baker. She pulled her brother Morris' cap lower on her head so that the brim of it shielded part of her face from view. Then, even while she was moving closer to the counter where the loaves were stacked in inviting abundance, she used the people around her as concealment. The people of this village were strangers to her, and because she and Gerald varied their market days weekly, sometimes traveling as many as ten miles to go to another town so that they would not attract attention with too frequent trips to the same village, it was unlikely that anyone would know them, or question their presence. Even if they did, the brother and sister had alibis concocted, with stories which did not include any references to Oldham or Katherine Stanley. They had been lucky so far.

The baker's eyes flickered over the people waiting for bread. He seemed more intent upon the money that they handed over than their faces, which was a good sign. Daisy edged her way to the side of the line. There were three people ahead of her.

Gerald, alert for the arrival of new customers, scanned the people around him to observe whether they were paying any attention to the slight, black-haired girl, her long hair caught up in a boy's cap to disguise her gender. No one was. It was a fine day and neighbors were chatting amiably to one another and oblivious to the presence of those they didn't know.

Daisy raised her hand to grip the loaf of bread on the end of the counter.

A man stepped up and handed the baker two coins for two loaves of bread.

As the baker gripped two loaves of bread in his huge hands to hand to the man in front, Daisy took hold of the loaf at the end and removed it.

The baker caught sight of the movement out of the corner of his eye.

"You thief!" he thundered, his dark face flushed with anger, dropping the loaves of bread he was about to hand to the customer.

The customer glanced about him. "Who you calling a thief!" he demanded.

He was speaking to no one, for the baker had come out from behind the counter and caught hold of Daisy's jacket, borrowed from Morris. He raised his hand to her.

Gerald, knowing that it was far more important to protect Daisy's identity than to avoid the risk of being discovered himself, pushed to the side of the stall and thrust his slender body against the baker's bulk.

"Run, Dais!" he shouted.

Daisy ran from the stall, fleeing as if she had grown wings. She only halted when she was beyond the stretch of stalls and was able to hide behind a ramshackle shed at the end of the street. She couldn't leave while Gerald might be in peril.

She waited until dusk fell, knowing that her sisters and brothers would be worried at the delay. But there was nothing more to be done but let the minutes and hours creep by until it was safe for her to make her way back to the market stalls, when the sellers had finished for the day and the street was devoid of its commerce.

Daisy decided that it would be better if she went back as herself, with her long, black hair braided. She couldn't do anything to alter the clothing she wore, but her hope was that no one would connect her with the one who had been accosted by the baker.

She walked quietly, but quickly, her heart beginning to beat faster as every step brought her closer into the center of town with no sign of her brother. But as she passed the school, she saw a crumpled heap on the side of the yard. The street was empty, everyone having gone to their homes to prepare and eat their evening meals.

"Gerald?" Daisy asked softly.

The heap stirred. "Daisy?'

Daisy went to her brother's side. A deep cut on his forehead had dripped blood onto his shirt, which was torn at the shoulder. His eye was bruised and swollen and would be black by morning, Daisy guessed. But what frightened her most was the difficulty he had in trying to sit up.

"He thrashed me proper, Daisy," Gerald admitted as he struggled to get up.

Daisy bent down and held out her hand. "I'll help you up. Then you can lean on me walking home."

It appeared that, although Gerald tried to mask his pain, he was having a difficult time of it. He finally was able to stand, but only when he put his arm around Daisy's waist and leaned against her for support was he able to take a step forward.

Daisy put her arm around his shoulder to bolster him. "We'll get home, Gerald, don't you fear," she encouraged him. As she offered a steady stream of reassurance, she couldn't help think on how desperate their situation was. They had a long walk until they reached the sanctuary they called home. Home was an abandoned mine shaft. How much more of this could they possibly endure?

THE LOST ONES MEET

The early part of the morning, when the sun was about to rise and the day about to begin, offered such promise that Perry almost forgot his dire circumstances. The morning birds had begun to chirp their songs as choirs of winged minstrels perched upon tree branches. The nocturnal animals faded back into their hiding places in the woods, knowing that the daytime was the province of the humans. It was a peaceful time of day, one that Perry cherished all the more because most of his hours would be spent in the netherworld of the mine, neither outdoors nor inside, but submerged in the dark confines of the earth.

Perry went, as he always did, to the brook, where he gathered water in a basin and washed. The water was cold, but it would soon warm up, he knew, after the sun had spent the day imbuing the brook with hours of warmth. He enjoyed his evening ablutions much more than the morning wash-up, although there was something bracing about the chilly assault of the water upon his skin. It certainly woke him up and prepared him for work.

Once he had eaten bread and cheese for breakfast, Perry set off for the mine as usual. Then he stopped and stared.

Not far ahead, no more than thirty yards, he saw the figure of a girl in a dress suddenly appear by one of the many overgrown hedges that had sprouted around the mine when the land was no longer cleared for farming or habitation. He blinked. The girl was gone.

Had he imagined it?

Perry was always the first one to arrive at the mine and he knew that he had plenty of time before he was required to show up for work, so he carefully made his way to the place where he'd spotted the girl. He found the place where she'd been seen, but no one was there now. The place itself looked to be vacant. But Perry's sharp eyes noticed a large, thorny overgrowth of hedgerows in the spot where the girl had disappeared. Mentally marking the spot in his mind, Perry continued on his way to work.

Throughout the day, as he worked below ground ignoring the customary aching in his shoulders and back as he bent his body to access the vein of black coal embedded in the mine, his mind traveled back over the sight from the morning. Perhaps because it was so uncommon for him to see anyone in the vicinity of where he was living, the image consumed his thoughts throughout the day. By the time he left the mine, he was intent upon one thing, and that was to find the mysterious girl who had appeared and then disappeared right before his eyes.

Perry paid particular attention, as he walked the distance from the mine to the rundown cottage he called home, to his solitude along the way. He sensed that there had to be a reason why the girl had been secretive in her movements, and he would not be the one to put her solitude at risk. Finding her had suddenly taken on an urgency that Perry could not have explained. The loneliness that had encompassed his life since leaving home had never seemed quite so oppressive as it did at that moment, when he beheld a girl who seemed more myth than human. Whatever his reasons, Perry wanted to know if he had a neighbor who might become a friend.

The hedgerow seemed to create a forbidding barrier to the outside world, although it appeared to be no more than more of the familiar overgrowth that characterized this section of the land where the mine had played out and the cottagers had been vacated as the miners moved nearer to where the dark veins were still surrendering their contents. But something didn't seem right. Perry reached his hand out to touch the hedgerow.

To his surprise, the vegetation moved. Perry shifted the greenery slightly with his hand. It moved more. He realized that what appeared to be a naturally growing hedgerow was no more than camouflage. But what was it concealing?

When he shifted the hedge more, he was surprised to see that beneath its thick green barrier, there was an opening leading into the ground below.

The abandoned mine! This was it, Perry realized with a feeling of exultation. The girl had not disappeared. This was where she intended to be.

How to reach out to her without frightening her? Why was she here? Was she hiding, and if so, from what? He had been unable, from that brief and startling glimpse, to tell whether she was a young girl or a woman. He had seen long dark hair and a dress, but unless he saw her from a closer range, he would never know more.

He peered into the opening to the abandoned mine. He wasn't foolhardy enough to risk going in, not when he had no idea of who else might be down in the mine besides the girl. For all he might know, the abandoned mine could be a hideout for a gang of thieves. Or worse.

He had to find out.

Perry sat down in front of the mine opening, once again thoroughly concealed by the untrimmed hedge. He leaned his forearms on his bent knees as if he were simply enjoying the pleasures of a quiet evening before dusk was overtaken by night. It was still light out; the sun was making a brilliant descent into the horizon. The leaves on the trees rustled slightly, but the wind was still as if all of nature were of the same mind to savor the tranquility of the hour.

Back in his cottage, his supper of bread and cheese and apples awaited him. He was hungry, not only for food but for the fact that breakfast and supper, unlike lunch, were not accompanied by the coal dust that laid a thin layer of grit over everything.

It struck Perry that if the girl was living in the mine, she too would be subject to the pervasiveness of coal dust. Whatever she had eaten would have that overlay upon it. The dust was inescapable. Perry could feel it in his hair, on his skin, so much a part of his work clothes that their original color was masked by a layer of gray.

He wondered if she sensed that he was outside the mine. Was it possible that she knew of his presence? The mine caverns were deep beneath the opening; it was unlikely that anyone knew he was there.

He stood up. He had an idea that might prove productive.

When he went to sleep, his slumber was deep and dreamless and he woke early before the dawn had broken. He packed a loaf of bread, a generous wedge of cheese, two red apples, and a slice of ham, items that he'd bought at the marketplace earlier in the week. He wrapped the food in a clean white cloth and tied a knot so that nothing would fall out.

The sun was just starting to rise by the time he reached the abandoned mine. The shadows covered him as he placed the white knapsack underneath the thorny tangle of hedge in front of the mine opening. The white cloth would catch the girl's eye, and yet the hedge would provide concealment in the unlikely event that anyone passed by.

Throughout the day, as he worked the seam before him, his shoulders hunched so that he could stay upright beneath the low ceiling of the mine, his feet damp from the water that was an inescapable factor in mining, Perry's mind left the cramped quarters and escaped outside. The image of the sunny landscape was more vivid to him, although it was distant, than the grime of the mine chamber. He could hear the picks striking into the coal seams all around him and on the other side of the wall. At the same time, the chirping birds in the trees, the lazy hum of the bees finding nourishment from the flowers, and all the sounds of nature were as vivid in Perry's mind as if he was out there. Images of the girl that he'd seen the previous day flitted into his thoughts in the same way that she'd darted into sight before. Had she found the food he'd hidden in the hedgerow? Would she appear?

What if the gift of food alarmed her and she left the mine? That possibility struck him with such immediacy that the remaining hours of his shift seemed interminable. When the whistle blew to signal the end of the workday, Perry was in a hurry to leave. The warm evening air greeted him when he came above ground and despite his sore shoulders and arms, he hurried on his way.

For a moment, he thought of stopping by the brook so that he could wash his face before going to the abandoned mine. Why was he concerned about how he looked, Perry derided himself. Why had this random appearance by a girl he didn't know captivated his thoughts so completely that he'd left food by the mine for her?

Probably, Perry decided as his long legs made swift work of the distance, it was because he was bored with his solitude. His life consisted solely of work and coming home to a rundown cottage. His diversions consisted of going to the marketplace to buy provisions for the week and sitting outside on a fallen tree while the birds, flowers, trees, and insects carried on their work all around him. It was peaceful, but it was lonely.

The sunshine was reluctant to depart from the day, even though the hour was moving into dusk. The abandoned mine was just ahead, still and silent as if no one had been near it. It was as if no one had ever been there, but Perry knew differently. He lived not far away, and he knew how isolated the abandoned mine area was. The thick overgrowth of grass and hedges created a natural barrier that offered protection for those within its green border. The birds who took refuge in the hedgerow trilled their songs in the daytime, but now, with the shadows of night on the way, they were silent, contributing to the impression that no one was here.

He took the last few yards with an impatient gait, eager to see what he might find when he reached the mine.

Perry peered down into the hedge. The white cloth was there, but folded neatly, the food gone from it. He bent lower.

Suddenly, without warning, a hand reached out from the hedge and gripped his wrist. "What do you want?"

It was a girl's voice. A young voice, but not that of a child. Coming from within the hedge.

"I only wanted to bring you food," he said. "Not to harm you. Come out, it's quite safe. I'm the only one here and I mean you no ill."

The hedgerow shifted. Perry already knew that the roots had been pulled up and the hedge was merely for camouflage.

He stepped back to give the girl room to emerge. He saw a gray skirt, and a battered shoe first. Then an arm, the sleeve marred by little tears that likely came from the thorns of the hedge. The hedge rustled more and then she appeared.

Even with the coating of dust that blurred the color of her dress and gave her black hair a silvery sheen that was at odds with her youthful skin and vivid dark eyes, she was striking to behold.

Those dark eyes were blazing "Why are you here?"

"I—I saw you yesterday morning," Perry stammered. He had not expected her to be so beautiful. The shabby attire and the coal dust could not conceal her loveliness. She was too thin, and the dress was loose upon her slender frame; still, her beauty gave her an incandescence that was arresting. "I thought—did you find the food I left?"

"I found it. Why did you leave it?"

Perry didn't know how to answer. *Because I saw you one minute, and you were gone the next and I was curious. Because I'm alone here and I couldn't help but welcome the thought that perhaps, someone else is nearby. Because I felt drawn to you, beyond anything that I can explain, and I wanted to see you. Because . . . who are you? I want to know more.*

"I thought you might be hungry," he said clumsily. "I wanted to help."

She looked up at him. She wasn't a diminutive woman, but her slight build made her seem even taller. Perry yearned to protect her, an impulse that he had never experienced before. There was something about her, something wondrous and mysterious, conjuring something new within him. At the age of almost twenty-one, Perry knew himself to be a full-grown man. Now, in the presence of this slip of a young woman, he felt awkward and gauche and uncertain.

Impulsively, Perry moved closer to her. Dying rays of the sun fell upon the blade in her hand, the knife he hadn't noticed until now.

"No closer," she warned, her features shuttering as if she were protecting herself from a threat. "I'll stab you if you do."

She raised the knife to emphasize her intentions.

Perry shook his head. This wasn't going at all the way he had hoped.

AN UNLIKELY FAMILY

Despite the presence of the knife, Perry did not feel that she was eager to use it. She reminded him of a woodland creature, shy and reclusive, reluctant to engage beyond boundaries that made her feel safe.

"I'm Perry Dalton," he said, hoping that he could ease her doubts by introducing himself, and receive her name in turn.

It might have worked. But he heard noise at the opening of the mine and then suddenly a blonde-haired girl appeared. She started when she noticed him, but wasted no time as she said, "Daisy, Gerald, he's burning up with fever, we don't know what to do—"

Darting as quickly as the woodland deer she brought to mind for Perry, the dark-haired girl—Daisy, she was called—went into the mine, following the other girl. Perry could not hang back. He went into the mine.

Mines were familiar to him now from his own employment. This abandoned mine, though, reminded him of a long-sealed tomb, where the air was stale and the atmosphere humid with the longstanding dampness inside.

They emerged into an open area where, once in its past, men had labored beneath the low ceilings to wrest coal from its craggy wall. The darkness of the area made it difficult to discern anything more than outlines. The two girls, knowing the layout of what appeared to be their living quarters, rushed over to a corner of the space and kneeled down.

"Gerald!" Daisy said to a form spread out upon the ground. "Gerald! Speak to me?"

Perry heard a voice uttering unintelligible words.

"Gerald!" Daisy's voice was choking on what Perry suspected was a sob. "Gerald, please, please—"

Perry wasn't sure what she wanted to ask of the incoherent figure on the floor, but he knew that the boy, and the others, had to leave the mine. It wasn't healthy.

He approached the girls and then realized, to his complete amazement, that there were other people in the room, clustered around the huddled body on the floor. There was a family living here!

Perry kneeled down on the ground beside the girls. "Daisy," he said, the urgency in his voice genuine. "If he's ill, the air in this mine won't let him heal. You can't leave him here."

"We don't have anywhere to go," she answered brusquely, her attention still focused upon the boy.

"You can come with me," Perry said. "I have a cottage. It's not much; it's rundown, but it's . . . Daisy, it's not an abandoned mine."

He saw her face turn to him. "Why should you care what happens to us?" she wanted to know.

He didn't have an answer to that, at least not an answer that made sense. "He's not going to get well like this," Perry replied. "Gather your things. We have a small walk, but it won't take us long to get there."

She was unsure. Perry could tell that she didn't know what to do. She feared staying there if it would make the boy sicken even more, but she didn't know whether she could trust him.

Another voice, a younger voice, piped up. "I don't like it here, Daisy; I want to go."

"How many of you are there?" Perry asked. The cottage had minimal furniture, so space would not be an impediment. It was nothing like a real home. But at least it wasn't an abandoned mine.

Perry picked the boy up from where he lay. He could feel that the boy's skin was fiery, and he knew that bringing the fever down would be a challenge. Lowering his head and hunching his shoulders, Perry began to walk forward.

He waited, the boy in his arms, until all the others had gathered up their belongings and met him at the entrance to the mine.

He counted six, including Daisy and the weak and feverish boy he was carrying. Two more girls, both with blonde hair, and two younger boys, also blond. All of them appeared to have missed too many meals, and living underground had given their skin a pasty cast beneath the coating of coal dust.

He could tell that Daisy was unsure about the decision to go with him.

"It'll be all right," he assured her softly as they walked, he and Daisy side by side in the lead, the others following behind with their belongings.

She didn't answer and they went the rest of the way in silence.

When they reached the cottage, he expected disparaging remarks regarding its condition. The front door was not attached to hinges and leaned forward in the entrance to keep animals from going in. There was no glass in the open squares that were windows. Perry had been working on the fallen beams in his spare time so that they had support. The result was rudimentary, but it served its purpose.

"I'll see what I can do about making beds," he said.

"We've gotten used to sleeping on the floor," Daisy told him wearily, as if a bed were something frivolous. She lifted her chin and studied him with an intense stare. "Where will we sleep?"

"The cabin has three rooms," he told her. "The kitchen, here, and the two back rooms. The boys can sleep in the room where I sleep. The girls can sleep with you."

Perry wondered why she had such a fierce expression on her face. "There's no door between the rooms. Just that opening between."

They were staying. She wouldn't be pressing about a door to separate the boys from the girls if she didn't intend to stay.

"We'll settle all that," he said in a calming voice. "First, we need to cool off this boy. I keep a barrel of rainwater outside. There's a basin on the shelf there. You've been nursing him through this?"

Daisy nodded. "As much as I can."

He didn't ask why they hadn't brought a doctor to see to the boy. For whatever reason they were living in an abandoned mine, they weren't in a position to welcome callers of any sort.

"There's mint growing wild in the back," he said.

The girl's face brightened. She knew what that meant. "I've been looking for mint to brew tea with," she said.

"I'll show you where it grows," he told her.

Daisy shook her head. "I know what it looks like. I'll find it. Can you light a fire?"

He pointed to the fireplace. It had seen better days, and there were bricks missing here and there, but he cooked food there with firewood from the fallen trees outside. "I'll start water boiling."

"Daisy, are we staying?" one of the younger boys wanted to know, tugging on her skirt.

Daisy looked at Perry, her countenance questioning.

"I hope you will," he said humbly. Inside, though, as he fetched firewood and poured rainwater into the battered pot he'd found in one of the other abandoned cottages, he felt as if he'd acquired a family and his heart was exultant.

First, though, they had to rescue Gerald from danger. Daisy shunned sleep as she worked through the night, replacing wet cloths on her brother's forehead. Perry stayed up through the night with her, refilling the basin with fresh water. The younger boys, Gus and Morris, fell asleep in the room where Perry slept. Vera and Eva, the two girls, stayed by their brother's side, although their eyelids were heavy with exhaustion.

Fortunately, the next day was Sunday and a day off for Perry. He usually went to church on Sundays but this was not a usual Sabbath. As Gerald's breathing eased and his fever was broken, Perry turned his attention to his inventory of supplies. If his cottage was to become home to the six newcomers, he would need more food. But when he suggested that Daisy go into the village to shop with the money he had saved, she demurred.

"Vera can go," she said. "She's fourteen."

As the days went by, Perry could not fault Vera's acumen at the market. She came home from her excursions with bread, cheese, potatoes, carrots, and apples; sometimes she was even able to stretch the funds Perry provided to buy a piece of meat. She, Daisy, and Eva would make a hearty soup that everyone enjoyed, with fresh bread heated over the fire and, sometimes, baked apples sprinkled with sugar.

It was a welcome change from his former solitude to come home from work to a cottage redolent with the aromas of food cooking over the fireplace, and bustling activity from everyone. Gerald was still recuperating from the fever, but his color was returning, and he was no longer bedridden. He assured Perry that it wouldn't be long before he'd be able to make himself useful around the cottage. But when Perry suggested that he might want to get work at the mine, Gerald was vague.

Perry didn't think too much about it. He could understand reluctance to go down into the internal caverns of the earth. He would have preferred work in the open air himself, but he'd been grateful for the mining and the pay it provided. There would be something else for Gerald when he was well again.

One night, after darkness had fallen, Perry went outside to sit on the fallen log by the cottage as was his habit. Sitting out in the darkness, with the secretive sounds of nature surrounding him, was surprisingly soothing and he cherished them. By the time he was ready to go back inside, the others would already be asleep and the candles doused.

He was surprised, therefore, when, several weeks after Daisy and her siblings had moved in, the front door—repaired now so that it opened and closed on hinges—opened and Daisy emerged. She moved so quietly that he might not even have noticed her in the darkness, but he had found, somewhat to his chagrin, that he was particularly attuned to the presence of Daisy.

"Do you mind if I sit a spell?" she asked, pausing at the door with the hesitance of the woodland deer she brought to mind.

As if he would ever mind the opportunity to spend time with Daisy.

Perry moved down a few spaces on the log so that she would have room. "Not at all, in fact, I'd welcome it. I'm usually out here alone and I'm the only one who gets to enjoy the peace of the night."

She sat down a circumspect distance apart from him, but nonetheless, nearby. The log was only so long, after all. Perry's spirits were heightened. He'd hoped for an opportunity like this, a chance to be alone with her, to talk and learn more about who she was. Perhaps this was that opportunity.

"I wanted to explain to you about Gerald," she said, folding the skirt of her dress neatly around her. She was economical in all her movements, Perry had noticed. Never a wasted motion and always graceful. Like a doe in the forest, watchful over her fawns, alert to possible danger.

Why had that image come to him? he wondered. What danger could there be? Gerald was well, or at least getting better. They were out of the mine, and they had shelter and food. They were safe.

"Is anything wrong? He seems to be faring quite well."

"Yes, yes, he is. Thank you for everything you've done. I wanted to explain why Gerald doesn't want to go into the mine."

"He doesn't have to be a miner. Myself, I'd rather be farming again, but that's for another time." One day, he hoped to return to farming, although there was little hope of it now, with his father so entirely under the control of his wife and her own plans for her own son. He'd been giving thought to Wales, of late. He'd never been there, but his mother was Welsh, and she'd often spoken of her family there and their farm. One day, perhaps . . .

"Our father was a miner. He died. The mine collapsed."

She spoke in a perfunctory way as if the explanation were necessarily brief. Perry sensed that she relayed these facts in that manner to avoid responding to the memory emotionally.

"I don't fault him, in any case, for not wanting to go down in the mine," Perry assured her. "Especially not if—your father, he's been gone long?"

The moon was like a lantern, spilling light below. It shone down on her as she nodded. "Ten years."

Ten years ago was long before he'd ever given a thought to working as a miner. "I'm sorry."

"He was a good man," she said.

"Your mother?" None of the family ever mentioned parents and Perry hadn't wanted to pry.

"We're orphans," Daisy said after a pause. "We're runaways. We were in an orphanage. We ran away. We were living in the mine so that no one would find us. We don't want to be a burden to you. But we can't work the way we'd like to. If someone from the orphanage saw us, they'd make us go back."

She spoke hurriedly, like the words had to be expelled from her lips because they were unsavory.

"Gerald and I, we were stealing to feed us all," she admitted. "Stealing's wrong. We know that. But we didn't know what else to do. We don't want to be a burden to you."

He didn't know how to tell her that having a family, of sorts, was payment enough. He liked having them in the cottage. He didn't feel isolated now. He had been putting money aside since he first started working and he was continuing to do so. It was true that he was spending more now on food, but he didn't begrudge anyone a meal, especially when they were all so industrious. The younger boys had gone scavenging around the other abandoned cottages and had come back with curtains, plates, a couple of blankets, even a little statue of a black and white dog that the girls had put on the windowsill in their sleeping room.

Everyone helped, everyone took part in whatever needed to be done. Daisy was a stickler for doing laundry once a week, then draping the wet clothes over the hedges so they would dry. Everything was done with an eye for keeping out of sight. To any chance passerby, there were no visible signs of occupancy, for the cottage was sheltered by trees and the hedgerows created a natural barrier against the outside world.

"We don't want to be a burden to you," Daisy said again.

"You're not a burden, Daisy. I'm pleased to have you. Only . . ." he hesitated.

Daisy stood up. "You want us to leave now that Gerald is better. I understand. We'll be gone—"

"Daisy, no! That's not what I was going to say." He reached out and took her hand, gently pulling her back down to sit on the log. "What I was going to say—and I hope you won't take this amiss—is that you and me living here—it wouldn't seem proper if someone should hear of it."

"We must take care that no one does hear of it," she said in alarm.

He hadn't released her hand when she sat. He could feel the tension in her light bones. He worked here, lived here, went to church in Oldham. Someone, at some point, would hear of it. He was a Christian. It wouldn't do for anyone to think that he was the sort of fellow who had a Sunday morning life and then the sort of life that might be misinterpreted the rest of the week.

"I'm asking you to marry me," he said in a low and uncertain voice. "It would make things fitting. We'd go on as we are," he assured her. "Only, your brothers and sisters really would be my family. You'd be my wife. What do you say?"

THE COMPLICATIONS OF MARRYING

Daisy knew little about young men and courtship. She heard the entreaty in his voice, and she wondered why he sounded as if he really wanted to marry her. She was clear-headed enough to recognize the authenticity of his concern. The lie she'd told him about being runaways from the orphanage troubled her, but it was necessary. Maybe marriage was necessary as well.

Perry was very kind. He'd shown himself to be that and more by taking in her family. He was very handsome as well, she thought, although that, of course, had nothing to do with the matter. He was offering matrimony as a matter of propriety. It seemed like too long since she'd been to church but she hadn't lost sight of the way a proper Christian was to behave. Her father's teachings had not left her during these last years.

"If you're sure," she said shyly. "If you're sure that you really want to marry me."

Perry's hand closed over hers. "I do want to marry you, Daisy. Truly I do."

Perry sounded sincere. He sounded as if he really did want to marry her. She couldn't imagine why, but there was something in his voice that made her feel pretty and, just for a moment, the decade of responsibility that had been hers since Papa's death eased, and she was a young woman with a handsome suitor.

Papa would have liked Perry, she thought later that night when she and Perry had finished chatting away as if they were longtime friends and she was in the bedroom with her sisters, all asleep on their bedrolls and oblivious to the rather remarkable circumstance which had just happened.

But getting married, Daisy found, wasn't simply a matter of agreeing to it. Perry wanted to be married in the church. The church at Oldham where he worshipped. That could never happen.

Daisy couldn't tell Perry that she had been born in Oldham and had, until the dreadful turn of events at the boarding house when she had unintentionally been the cause of her mother's lover's death, walked the miles to worship at the church there. Now that weeks had gone by since she'd appeared in the village, she hoped that the folks she'd once called friends and neighbors had forgotten all about the blighted Stanley family.

Once again, she called upon a lie.

"We can't be married in Oldham, Perry," she told him one evening not long after he had proposed. It was nighttime and she and Perry were outside, perched upon the log. The others were in bed. Perry had broken the news of the engagement and the children were excited about the news. The boys were happy to have a brother; now, Morris said, there would be more boys than girls. The girls had been pleased too; Perry was a favorite and had soon won their affection with his affable ways and his kindness.

"Why not? It's a fine church."

She didn't tell Perry that she knew the church well. Had her life turned out differently, she would have expected to marry there.

"The orphanage," she said promptly.

"The orphanage is a good twenty miles away," he argued. 'It's not likely that anyone in the church would turn your brothers and sisters in."

"Word would get out. Folks talk, even when they don't mean to. Gerald was an apprentice, he ran away from a cruel master." Silently, Daisy prayed that she would be forgiven for her lies. "Vera was to be sent into service to a household with—"

She halted. What sort of vile master could she concoct for this one?

She didn't need to. "A master who doesn't leave the servant girls alone?" Perry guessed, his tone grim, when she was unable to finish her sentence.

"Yes! Yes, that was it. Vera wouldn't go. We didn't want her to go. Can't we get married somewhere else?"

"I suppose we could get married in Henshaw's Ford," he said. "It's a good ten miles from here, farther away from the orphanage."

Daisy was saddened at the realization that Perry would sacrifice getting married in the church he'd taken to when he moved to the area because of her. She resolved that she would be the very best wife she could ever be, to make up for all that he had lost. He had told her about his own circumstances and the farm he'd left because his father was under the thumb of Perry's stepmother.

Daisy felt sorrow for Perry to have sacrificed so much. But she had learned that her husband-to-be was an enterprising young man who did not waste time on what he could not change.

Several nights later, over supper, the family learned that he had again been busy making plans to better their lot.

He'd been late coming home, something unusual for Perry, who was eager to return to the cottage after the long hours at the mine. As he sat down at the table with its seven unmatched chairs, he surveyed their faces.

"I've found a better place for us," he said.

"You mean we're moving?" Daisy stood stock still, the pan of sausages frozen in her hand.

He beamed. "Yes, indeed. I walked home the long way tonight, and what should I see but a bonny-looking cottage on the edge of the Olsen estate."

"The Olsen estate."

"Yes, Mr. Olsen."

"He owns the mine," Daisy said tonelessly.

"Yes, he does," Perry nodded jovially. "That cottage is bigger than this one, and in good shape. It needs a bit of work, but I went up to the house and asked to speak to the steward. It turns out that they'd like the cottage to be occupied before winter sets in. I said my wife and I and our kin—" Perry winked at the sisters and brothers who would soon be his own relatives as well—" were looking for a bigger place. I said we'll keep the place neat and clean and I'm able to lend a hand at harvest time or with any chore that needs doing outside of my hours at the mine. The steward said that sounded fair to him and when did I plan to move in?"

Daisy wasn't at all sure that living on the Olsen estate was going to be a propitious move. "The orphanage," she reminded him. She had already alerted her siblings to the subterfuge she had employed to explain their unusual circumstances.

Perry waved a dismissive hand. "The Olsen family only have doings with the others in their set," he said, "and the tenants aren't likely to be telling tales about folks they don't even know. They're farming folk and they have little to do with mining folk."

Perhaps it would be all right, Daisy told herself. Perhaps no one would ever need to know the truth. She had never given their real surname to Perry, who thought her name was Daisy Wilbur. It was another lie, Daisy knew, and lying was a sin. She wondered wearily if Mrs. Calloway's assurance was the truth as God saw it. *Sometimes in life, you have to choose between two sins, one the lesser and one the greater.*

∽

They had moved into the cottage at the edge of the Olsen estate. Despite Daisy's worries, she found that Perry was correct in his estimation that they would be safe. The tenants were not unfriendly, but they kept to themselves, minding their own business and working their fields. This time of year, they were especially busy with the harvesting. She was not averse to letting Gus, Morris, and Eva work with others hired on for harvesting; they had been too young when the Stanleys left Oldham for anyone to recognize them. Even Vera, who had only been four when the family moved to the boarding house, was very different now from the child she'd been then, but Vera kept busy in the cottage and liked helping Daisy with the cooking, cleaning, sewing and laundry.

With all of them, theirs was a large household and Daisy was glad of her sister's assistance. Just as she was glad that the younger children were helping by bringing in wages. She knew that Perry was sincere when he said they were no burden to him. Still, she felt better that they could also provide. Daisy didn't think it was right to be wife to a man who was willing to take on her siblings if she had nothing to offer. The younger Stanleys were proud to be earning, especially since it meant that Vera had more money for market day and was more likely to indulge in treats on occasion.

For the first time in ever so long, Daisy was happy. She was happy, too, at the thought of marrying Perry, although she never disclosed her feelings to him. Theirs was a marriage for the convenience it provided. She understood that. Perhaps, someday, they could be a real husband and wife. In the meantime, they were a family and that was reason enough to be grateful to God.

The wedding day dawned on a beautiful autumn morning when the air was still filled with the lingering warmth of summer, but with an added flavor in the breeze that came from the tangy scent of the apples rich and ripe in the orchards. Some of the farmers had begun their cider-making early with the windfalls and the scent of apples layered the air.

"I wish we could go," Eva said wistfully.

"I wish that too," Daisy said, giving her youngest sister a kiss. "But we'd be too easily noticed if we all went together. Someone might see us and..."

She didn't need to finish. Someone might see and bring to mind the six Stanleys who had vanished after the death of the sailor in Mrs. Calloway's boarding house. No, it wasn't worth the risk.

"Besides," Daisy said, pragmatic once more, "it's a long walk to Henshaw's Ford. By the time we get there and get married, we'll be turning around to come back, and it'll be going on for nighttime."

"Someday, we'll have a horse and cart," Vera said confidently. "We'll ride to wherever we need to go."

She and Eva laughed happily at the future they were envisioning. As Daisy took her best Sunday dress down from one of the wooden hooks on the wall where all their dresses hung, she thought again how happy they all were. Thanks to Perry and his willingness to take care of them, she thought.

She realized that the girls were giggling and looked up.

"Close your eyes, Daisy," Vera commanded.

"Put that old dress away," Eva ordered, echoing her sister's tone just as she had done when they were little.

"It's my best dress! It's my wedding dress. I washed it especially for today."

"Close your eyes."

"Why—oh, very well," Daisy said, humoring her sisters. They certainly were in a silly mood today, but she enjoyed the levity. There hadn't been much laughter in their lives until they'd left the mine and moved to the old miner's cottage. Now, they were in a bigger, better-maintained tenant cottage on the Olsen estate. Next spring, they'd be planting their own field, keeping some of the harvest for their own use and rendering what they owed to Mr. Olsen. Gerald was excited at the thought of being able to farm; he was learning a lot already just from talking to Perry, who missed being outside to work the land.

Perhaps next spring, Daisy thought, Perry might be able to leave the mine. She dreaded the thought of him being underground all day long. Her memory of Papa's death was still vivid in her mind, and she thought that if something happened to Perry, she didn't know how she'd manage. She'd—

"Now you can open them!" Eva announced.

Daisy opened her eyes. Vera was holding a new dress in front of her. It was a simple design. The skirt reached to Vera's ankles, and the bodice had a round neckline. The sleeves were full and ended at the elbow. What was remarkable about the dress wasn't the pattern. It was the color. Instead of the usual drab gray, dull blue, plain black colors that were customary among the females of the mining community, this dress was a lovely light green. The color of spring when the first shoots of the season began to push forth from the ground. It was a hopeful color, not one subdued by the dust of the coal.

Daisy stared. "It's lovely," she said, her features puckered in a frown.

"Don't you like it?" Eva asked, crestfallen.

"Yes, but—where did it come from?"

Vera brought the dress to her sister. "Perry gave me money to go into the village to buy fabric and thread and buttons," she said. "He said you ought to have a special dress for your wedding day. Me and Eva have been sewing on it, in secret, all this time and you never guessed."

"How on earth did you hide it?" Daisy reached out a finger to touch the soft cotton. The green was so vivid that she felt as if something would grow from the cloth any minute.

"Remember when we were sewing the bedsheets?" Eva asked. "We had the dress underneath it. We'd sew on laundry day and every time you went outside, one of us went with you and the other stayed inside to sew on the dress."

"How did I miss that?"

"You miss a lot of things, Daisy," Vera said. She spoke in a light tone, but her face was serious. "You're so busy looking after us that you don't see what's right in front of your face. Perry loves you. We can all see it. You're the only one who doesn't see how much he loves you."

"We're getting married so that there's no impropriety," Daisy insisted, lowering her head to study the stitching on the dress so that her sisters wouldn't see her blushes.

"I know that's what he told you. I know that's what you think. But he loves you. One day, you'll see that for yourself." Vera sounded old and wise beyond her years.

"Now, come on and put on the dress!" Eva exclaimed in excitement, dispelling the seriousness of Vera's words.

Daisy was relieved at the change of subject. Whatever had made Vera come up with such an outlandish notion? Perry in love with her . . . why, it was utter fancy!

THE WEDDING

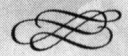

D aisy didn't pull back when Perry took her hand after they left the church. He didn't relinquish it as they began their journey back to their cottage. He held her hand up, the better to see his mother's wedding ring on her finger. He'd followed his father's instructions, and found the girl who would, like his mother, bring him love.

"Mr. and Mrs. Perry Dalton," he said. "Daisy Dalton." He turned his head to look at her. "What do you think of it?"

"I think it sounds very fine," she told him.

"I do too."

They shared a smile and walked on. Perry hoped they'd get home before dark; the clouds appeared full and threatened rain. The lovely morning weather had lasted through their long walk to Henshaw's Ford, but autumn was unpredictable. Once they reached the cottage, they'd be all right. The roof didn't leak, and the windows were tight.

"At least now, we won't have to worry about the winter," Daisy said as if she had been reading his thoughts. "We'll be snug in the new cottage."

Perry smiled at her. Her fingers were small, enclosed in his strong hand. Even with all the washing and cleaning and cooking that she did, her hands were still softer than his miner's hands, which were calloused from long hours wielding a pickaxe. The new dress looked right fine on her, too. His heart swelled with pride at how fine she looked in it. She didn't look like a miner's wife, beaten down and drab. She looked as elegant as a lady of the manor.

He said so, feeling more comfortable in praising her now that she was his wife. "Green, now, that's the color for you, Daisy."

"It's far too pretty for the likes of me," she said.

"One day, you'll have a dress for every day of the week," he promised.

"I don't know how we'd ever afford such a thing," she disputed his claim. "I don't know anyone who has that many dresses. Most women have one dress for everyday and one for church on Sunday."

It was an opening to the subject he longed to bring up. "One day, Daisy, I want you to come to church with me. When you're not afraid any more about the orphanage," he said quickly after spotting the frightened expression in her dark eyes.

"I don't know when that will be, Perry," she said.

"One day. When the lads are grown, you won't have to fret for them being found," he said. "That's only in a few years."

He wished that she didn't take on that skittish, frightened look that made him think again of a frightened doe ready to dart away at the first indication of a threat. To ease her alarm, he changed the subject.

"I don't know that I'm of a mind to stay in England all my days," he said. "What do you think? Would you be against it?"

"Against leaving England? Where would we go?"

His heart warmed to hear her include herself in the question of where they might go instead of staying where they were. He knew that where Daisy went, her family went. That made the prospect even more appealing.

"I've told you of my mother's people in Wales," he said. "My grandfather has a farm. My mother talked of it often. She was fond of Wales. I have an uncle, her brother, who lives in Manchester. We didn't see each other often but we got on well."

"He doesn't want to go back to Wales?"

"He's settled in Manchester now with an English family. That's how my father met my mother. She was visiting from Wales. Her brother's wife's family lived near our farm, the Dalton farm. My father and mother took to each other from the start."

The way I've taken to you, Daisy, Perry thought but didn't say. *Maybe it runs that way in us Daltons.*

"Wales," Daisy mused as if it were something to ponder. "I've never thought of living there or anywhere. But I'd not object," she told him. Her face was bright with a beautiful smile.

"You know," he said, "The Welsh are known for their singing."

"Are they now?" she answered back. "Judging by other Welshmen?"

"I'll sing and you can tell me what you think of it."

He broke into an old ballad that his mother had sung to him, his voice ringing out as he and Daisy walked along the dirt road. Now and then, a wagon passed by, and the driver would give the pair an interested glance, finding entertainment in the sight of a couple singing their way to their destination.

"It's very pretty," Daisy said when he finished singing. "But what do the words mean?"

"Hanged if I know," he replied. "My mother sang it in Welsh, but I never knew the words."

"How will we get on in Wales if none of us speaks Welsh?" she asked him.

"My mother spoke English and Welsh. Lots of them do," he said, hoping it was so. It was something to ask Uncle Ivor, if he saw him again in Manchester one day. "Now it's your turn," he told her. "You sing a song."

Daisy protested that she didn't sing well.

"Very well, then," Perry told her. "We'll sing together. Name a song."

Daisy looked very uncertain. Her vulnerability in this small thing, when she was so staunch and strong in so many other aspects—her protectiveness toward her siblings, her willingness to work hard, her ability to do without—invigorated his own determination to take care of her.

"I don't know many songs," she said. "I only know hymns."

"I know hymns too," he replied promptly. "Go on, see if we know the same ones."

She opened her mouth to sing, brought forth a note, and then shook her head. "I can't."

"Of course, you can, Daisy," he said. He stopped along the side of the road and took both her hands in his. "We'll sing them together. Come on now, give it a try. Do you know the Queen's favorite hymn?"

Daisy shook her head.

"I reckon you know this one."

He released her other hand, and they began walking along the road again.

"'Rock of Ages, cleft for me, let me hide myself in Thee;

Let the water and the blood, from Thy wounded side which flowed,

Be of sin the double cure; save from wrath and make me pure.'"

A wagon drove by, the husband and wife in the seat, a brood of children in the back of the wagon. They joined in as they passed, and the notes of the second verse could be heard as they rode by.

"You see," Perry encouraged her. "Now it really is your turn."

"Only if you sing with me," she insisted. "Then I'll sing."

Perry felt his heart beating like the hammer of a blacksmith in a fiery forge. "It's better anyway, when we sing together," he said quietly.

He started off with the third verse and she, tremulously, joined in. Her voice was sweet and pure, softer than his, but blending well, so that as they sang, the verses had a fullness they would have been deprived of had the couple not sung in tandem.

They sang hymns the rest of the way home, and when the clouds, which had been threatening to open up all afternoon, finally did so as evening faded into night, Perry and Daisy burst out laughing. They ran the rest of the way to their cottage, confounding the other Stanleys, who could not conceive of what was so amusing about being drenched by a downpour.

∼

Having heard Daisy's sweet singing voice, Perry was more determined than ever to persuade her to join him at church. He decided that he would do it in stages. The first stage was to share the goings-on of the church folks when he came home on Sundays, to awaken in her a curiosity about the people who had been, until he met Daisy and her siblings, the only sort of family he'd had since arriving in the village.

He began with mention of the sermon. Daisy listened eagerly as if she were starved for the word of God. The others listened as well, but it was Daisy who gave avid attention to Perry.

Perry spread butter on the bread that was still warm from baking. Milk was easy to come by on the Olsen estate, and Perry had borrowed the butter churn from the steward so that Vera could use it. Bread and butter, and vegetable soup bountiful with thick chunks of potatoes and carrots made a nourishing lunch on a rainy autumn day when the days were beginning to foretell the chill to come as November beckoned.

"The banns were announced for Annie Larkin," he went on. "She's to wed one of the mining lads."

"Annie Larkin," Daisy repeated slowly.

"Yes, she's one of nine. Mrs. Larkin, well, she has a big family. Her husband can't go down in the mines any more for the coughing. He's not faring well. Mrs. Larkin takes in laundry to make ends meet. I reckon that it'll be easier on them now, with one less mouth to feed."

He went on, talking of the others in the congregation, the births, baptisms, engagements and weddings, and deaths that had taken place. He hoped that, even though the names would be unfamiliar to Daisy, she would take an interest in the lives of the others in the area. But she seemed to fall silent after a bit and he wondered if perhaps she had no interest in people she didn't know.

It was all well and good, Perry thought to himself the following Sunday as he removed his cap and entered the church, to be fully occupied with one's family. Still, it would do Daisy good if she met other people. There was fellowship to be enjoyed with others. She didn't need to be so busy all the time with the work that was to be done; he wouldn't have minded if she became interested in churchgoing and from here, developed a circle of friends with like interests.

He made a point, before and after the service, to listen even more closely to the conversations of the churchgoers so that he would have stories to bring home for lunch.

Mrs. Larkin was talking to several of the other ladies; he could hear her voice over the din of the other conversations. She was talking about her daughter's upcoming wedding. With the thought of his own wedding to Daisy fresh in his mind, Perry paid close attention. Daisy would enjoy hearing about another girl's wedding, he thought.

Mrs. Larkin was shaking her head. "Annie dearly wanted for the Stanley children to come to her wedding," she said. "I'd like to see them all too. It's been too long since they suddenly stopped coming for church. I went to Sadie Calloway's, that's where they moved to after the mine collapse that killed Mr. Stanley. Katherine Stanley, she's in a bad way," Mrs. Larkin disclosed. "You remember how pretty she was?

Several of the women encircling Mrs. Larkin acknowledged the woman's beauty.

"She's in a bad way," Mrs. Larkin said, her expression disapproving. "I don't wonder but it's because of her that Daisy did what she did."

Perry's attention was captured when he heard the name Daisy. Of course, it would be another Daisy, it was not an uncommon name.

"What did Daisy do?" another woman asked. "She was always an obliging child. If you ask me, she was more mother to those other five children than Katherine was, even though she was no more than a child herself."

"It pains me to say this," Mrs. Larkin said, "but Daisy's done murder."

"Murder!" the women exclaimed in unison. They were clustered in the church yard and even though the temperature was falling, no one was going to hurry home now, not with news of this nature.

"Sadie said she still didn't know what happened, but it seems that Katherine had taken a lover, a sailor man. I wouldn't be surprised if the sailor took a shine to Daisy, she had grown into a pretty thing, with that black hair and eyes that looked like they were near black too."

Perry felt himself growing rigid as if Mrs. Larkin's words had turned him to stone. It couldn't be his Daisy. There were plenty of black-haired, dark-eyed girls in England and small wonder if a portion of them were named Daisy. But he listened with even more rapt attention now as Mrs. Larkin went on.

"This sailor fellow, it seems he fell to his death down the stairs. Katherine blamed Daisy for it. Next thing you know, Sadie told me, the Stanley children are gone. All of them: Daisy, Gerald, Vera, Eva, Gus, and Morris, the youngest. No one knows where they headed off to, but Sadie said the constable is looking for Daisy."

Perry heard the women expressing their regrets and even though it sounded as though their sympathies were with Daisy, Perry had heard enough. His eyes filled with tears as he blindly strode through the church yard, stricken by what he had learned. There was no going back from the truth. He was married to a murderess.

THE PAST RETURNS

Having lunch waiting for Perry when he came home from church was something that Daisy particularly enjoyed. Even when the meal was no more than bread and soup, it mattered that the bread was baked over their own fireplace, and the soup was rich with the onions and vegetables and, sometimes, a small piece of meat that added flavor to the broth. She and her sisters had made jam with the berries that grew wild; today's Sunday lunch would have an added treat: bread and strawberry jam to follow the soup.

Life was very fine these days, Daisy mused as she placed spoons by the bowls on the table where they would eat. They were warm inside their cottage, with no fear of the winter to come. The younger Stanleys had made a good impression during the harvest and were often paid to do other small chores around the estate. Vera was as frugal as ever when she shopped for their needs, but even so, there was money to put aside for savings. Perry refused to take their savings; he said they contributed enough with their wages and the small amount that they saved was for them to use as they saw fit.

He was a good man, Daisy knew. She wished that she could make a clean breast of things and let him know the truth about why she could not go to church, or go to the village, or share in the life of the community. She thought often of the fate that was due her for the death of the sailor. Part of her knew that the proper thing to do would be to turn herself in to the law and accept the consequences.

But she just couldn't do that, even now, when her sisters and brothers had Perry to look after them. She had not meant to kill the sailor, even if she had been the unwitting cause of his death. She didn't want to hang for the death of a man who had intended to harm her. She didn't want to hang at all, especially now, when her life was beginning to take on a happiness the likes of which she hadn't known since she gave Papa his kiss good-bye as he went off to the mine for the last time.

Daisy stood back and surveyed the table. Perry would be home soon. He would come in, hang his cap on the wall hook, take off his jacket, and then breathe in the aromas of the food that was waiting. He would say, "I must be doing something right for God to reward me with good things to eat after church." He would—

She heard the sound of his footsteps nearing the cottage. The boys would be coming home soon; they were helping to chop up a tree that had fallen during a storm. They were promised a load of firewood for their labors, firewood that would come in handy for the fireplace in the winter. The girls were in the bedroom, sewing; they would hear him at the door and join the others for lunch.

The door opened. Daisy smiled and prepared to greet him.

But this wasn't the Perry who came home from church with a glad heart. She didn't know this man, his face dark with anger, his features stern.

"Perry?"

"Why didn't you tell me you'd murdered a man?"

His voice was almost incoherent with the layers of fury that thickened each word. Daisy stared at him in disbelief. What had he learned? Who would have told him about the sailor at Mrs. Calloway's boarding house? He had gone to church—if anyone at church knew that she was here, she and her family were in danger.

"What did you tell them?" Daisy cried out.

They stood across from each other, the table laden with plates and cups, a plate of bread, and bowls of butter and jam in between them like a referee. Hearing their voices, the girls had emerged from their room. None of the customary mirth was in their countenances as they stared at their sister and her husband.

"Perry, did you tell the folks at church that we're married?"

"I never said a word! How could I, Daisy? I was learning about the woman I thought I knew. They spoke of a Daisy Stanley who'd been a mother to her sisters and brothers, an obliging child, of a mother who'd gone bad, and a sailor that Daisy murdered. Oh, they were very sympathetic. As if you were justified in what you did."

"She was," Gerald and his brothers had entered the cottage quietly, but Perry's back was to the door and he had heard nothing of their arrival.

Gerald closed the door. "Daisy didn't mean for him to die," he went on, his dark eyes, so like Daisy's, fixed upon the man who was as much father as brother to the Stanleys now. "You don't know what it was like in those days. Mama—she wasn't herself. It all fell upon Daisy. Mama, the men from the pub—the sailor, he noticed Daisy. He meant her no good. He fell down the stairs. We lit out of there as soon as we could. We came here, to the mine. You found us."

Gerald relayed the story simply, in a voice devoid of emotion. Only his eyes seemed to recall the tumult of that terrible night.

"I didn't know Daisy was a fugitive! I didn't know the law was looking for a murderess! You told me you were runaways from an orphanage!" Perry flung the words at her. "I wanted to help."

"You did help," Daisy told him. "You saved Gerald's life. He'd have died if we'd stayed down in the mine. You saved us all."

"Don't you know what you've done, Daisy?" Perry leaned his arms on the table. "I thought we were a Christian household. I thought we were going to do right by one another and by God. Now I learn that the woman I thought I knew, the woman I thought I'd be married to for the rest of my life, is wanted for murdering a man. How could you sleep at night with that on your conscience?"

"Perry," Vera came forward. "You can't accuse Daisy without understanding what happened that night."

"Is a man dead or is he not?" Perry demanded.

"Yes, he's dead!" Vera replied, her blue eyes blazing. "And I'm right glad he is, for if he was alive, it would mean he'd had his way with Daisy, and no one to defend her or protect her or even speak up for her. Our mother, our own mother, turned against Daisy, when it was our Daisy who kept us together as a family, saw to it that we had something to eat, and taught us the Bible—"

"Did she teach you that the Bible says 'Thou shalt not kill'?" Perry asked.

Vera, the most outspoken of them all, looked at Perry with a weary gaze. "I'd have done him in myself if he'd hurt our Daisy. You don't know anything of what we went through, or how much Daisy did for us. We're all grateful to you for the good you've done, but we won't have our sister spoken to as if she's a dangerous criminal."

"If you've got an explanation for what happened with that sailor," Perry said, his voice still thick with anger, but frosted now with a cold tone that made his words sound like a sentence from a judge. "I'll listen to it. But first, first, you must be willing to surrender yourself to the police and trust to God to find you innocent. You can't live here under false pretenses. You can't expect me to tolerate you raising up your sisters and brothers that I've come to love as if they were my brothers and sisters too, and you a murderess wanted by the law. You'll have to choose. You have until tonight."

He stood up from the table. "I loved the woman I thought you were, Daisy."

Now his voice was sorrowful. He started to speak again but could not go on. He went out the front door.

Daisy knew she had no time to spare. Still, she couldn't help but pause for a moment to stare at the table set for a meal no one wanted to eat. There had been a time when she thought the greatest problems she faced were finding food and shelter for her family. Now she had to leave both.

"Where are you going, Daisy?" Gerald asked as Daisy turned from the kitchen.

"I have to leave," she said. "I need to be on my way before he returns. If he comes back with the police—"

"Perry would never do that to you," Eva protested.

But Vera was already following Daisy into the bedroom the sisters shared. "Where will you go?" she asked matter-of-factly as she began to take Daisy's clothes from the hooks on the wall, to fold them and pack them into a knapsack.

"I'll go to London. I can hide there where no policeman will find me."

"London!" Morris repeated.

Vera was nodding. "That's safest."

"Why can't we go with you?" Eva wanted to know, her face crumpling at the prospect of being without Daisy.

"If they're looking for Daisy," Gerald said, swallowing the lump in his throat before he could continue, "they'll expect to see us with her. We've always been with her."

Daisy nodded. Her siblings understood. Like her, they'd grown up dealing with life as it was, not as they wished it could be. The weeks with Perry had been among the happiest in all their lives, but happiness didn't seem to be of a mind to stay.

"How will we know if you're all right?" Gerald asked.

"I'll find a way to send word to you—maybe money, if I can come up with a means of sending it."

Gerald ran to the vase on the windowsill where the boys stored their earnings from working on the Olsen fields. "Take this," he said, turning the vase upside down and letting the coins tumble onto the bed. "You'll need money in London."

"I can't take that," Daisy said, aghast at the idea. "You've all worked hard for that money."

"We'll work hard again, Daisy," Gerald told her as he filled a thick woolen sock with the coins. "But London takes money. You'll need it more."

The others nodded solemnly. "We couldn't have a moment's peace, Daisy, if we thought you were in London with nothing."

"What will you do?"

"I'll find work," Daisy said. "There's plenty of work to be had in London, I'm told."

"Daisy, aren't you afraid?" Gus asked her. Her brother's blue eyes were enormous at the thought of going so far away and to such a place. He'd never been there, none of them had, but the storied city was the source of many tales.

"Not a bit," Daisy lied. She tied a kerchief around her head, covering the thick hair she'd pinned up.

"Daisy, what about your wedding dress?" Eva questioned, seeing the pretty green frock hanging on the hook.

Daisy shook her head. "I won't need it if I'm working in the scullery," she said.

"What will we do with it?"

"Leave it there," Vera said, her voice hard. "Leave it there so Perry sees it and thinks on what he's done."

Daisy saw her oldest brother and sister exchange glances and she knew that they too would be leaving the snug, cozy cottage on the Olsen estate. She couldn't blame them, but she dreaded the thought of them being out in the cold with winter coming on.

"You'll have a care, won't you?" Daisy said as she pulled on her shawl. "Don't be reckless, now."

"We'll look after them," Gerald assured her. "Just like you've always done."

"Oh, Daisy," Eva cried out, running to her sister and hugging her.

No one wanted to cry, but there was no escaping it. They all enclosed her in a family embrace that attested to the love they had for her and the loyalty that welded them together.

"Mind you say your prayers every night," Daisy told them when she was ready to go. It was still daylight out but that would help her find her way.

Vera wrapped the loaf of bread from the table into a cloth and tucked it into Daisy's knapsack. "We'll pray for you, and you pray for us," she said. She poured water from the pitcher into a glass flask and found a niche in the knapsack for it. "You'll get thirsty, walking," she said.

The two sisters hugged. Neither one cried. Vera was learning, as Daisy had learned years ago, that it was necessary to hide the feelings that hurt the most. The others needed to see strength, not weakness.

Morris began to follow Daisy out the door, but Vera held him back, her arms folded over him. "No," she said.

Daisy nodded. Vera would know what to do, and so would Gerald. With God's guidance, they would manage. As for Perry—she had to leave without saying goodbye. Nor could she tell him she loved him. It had been true for some time, but she'd never said so. Now she never would, even though it was still true.

ALONE

Perry was not sure what to expect when he returned to the cottage, many hours later, but he was not prepared for the cottage to be dark, the fire out, the table bare. He had never walked into the cottage without someone there to greet him and the warmth of the fire easing the chill from his body, while the aroma of the meal on the hearth wafted through the rooms like a promise that all was well.

"Gerald?" he called as he lighted a candle and carried the candlestick to the bedroom where the boys slept. "Morris? Gus?"

The hooks where their clothes had hung were bare. They didn't own a lot, but they had taken their own belongings. As he went into the girls' room, he saw evidence of the same. What was Perry's remained. They had heeded the strict code that they had been raised with, the Daisy code.

She had hated stealing from the marketplace, but she had done it with a prayer for forgiveness all the while, Perry knew.

The girls' clothes were gone, just like their brothers'. Then he saw it, the green dress she'd worn on her wedding. It hung in solitude, with the other garments gone. Perry was overcome when he saw the dress and all that it had promised on the day Daisy had become his wife.

Perry sank to the floor and pressed his hands to his face. He couldn't stop the tears that flooded his eyes. Every dream he'd cherished came from loving Daisy. With her, he'd been confident that dreams would one day come true as long as he worked hard and did right by the Lord and took care of the family that had become his own. Now they were gone, all of them, and Daisy was gone, and dreams were barren.

He wasn't taking care of them now. They were on their own, and winter was coming. What would they do? If only Daisy—

"If only Daisy what?" Perry asked himself bitterly. "If only Daisy wasn't a murderess?"

He couldn't have lived with her, knowing the truth as he now did. Murder was a crime. If she'd confessed her crime, there would have been a trial, but she might have been found innocent. Perhaps she did kill the sailor, but her brothers and sisters had intimated that Daisy was not at fault, that the sailor had provoked the incident by his actions toward Daisy. Their mother, it seemed, had sided with the sailor and blamed her daughter.

Had he been hasty in accusing Daisy? No one had denied the charge. His intention had not been to drive them all from the cottage. They were his family now, and Daisy was his wife. He had thought that if Daisy presented herself to the law, the police would seek evidence to find out the truth. He had expected her brothers and sisters to stay at the cottage so that he could look after them while justice played out through the legal channels, as it was supposed to do.

Daisy was no murderer. Why hadn't she told him the truth about herself, her mother, her family, and why they were in flight? Why had she spun that tale about the orphanage?

He ought to have sensed that there was a reason why she was so reluctant to be in the company of others. She had been willing to live a life of concealment, just so that she could stay with her family and look after them. She had looked after him as well, in her woman's way. She had sewn buttons on his shirt and gotten up early in the morning to prepare breakfast so that he set off for the mine with food in his belly and a packed lunch for later. Because of Daisy, he had a family now, and a home. Now, he had lost it all.

Perry exhaled slowly and tried to think. Mrs. Larkin had given the same impression as Daisy's brothers and sisters.

Mrs. Larkin was a kind woman, but she was sensible. She wouldn't fall for the blandishments and excuses that a guilty person might offer. Perhaps she was the key to this.

∾

After his work ended the next evening, Perry was in no hurry to return to the cottage. Instead, he walked to the Larkin cottage.

"Why, Perry Dalton," Mrs. Larkin greeted him when she opened the door. "Come on in, lad, before the chill takes us all."

She was the only one at home except for her husband. Mr. Larkin wasn't in the room, but Perry could hear him coughing from another part of the house. He saw folded piles of clothing on the table and realized that the Larkins were probably delivering clean laundry to other cottages.

That gave him an idea. "Mrs. Larkin, I wonder if you'd be able to do my laundry? I didn't bring it with me, but I'd be grateful if you'd take me on as one of your clients."

"Bless us, I'll be glad to do it," she said as she filled a kettle with water from a pitcher and put it on the stove to heat. "You'll take a cup, sure?"

"I'd be glad to," he said, wondering how the Larkins could even afford tea with Mr. Larkin no longer able to work in the mine. Maybe the laundry business was sufficient for their means. "Mrs. Larkin," he said when she handed him a cup. "On Sunday, you were talking about a murder?"

Mrs. Larkin sat down, took out her sewing box, and began to thread a needle. "I wasn't gossiping, although it must have sounded as I was."

"No, it didn't sound like gossip. I'm new to Oldham, and I was curious."

"The murder didn't take place in Oldham proper," she corrected him as she began to attach a button to one of the shirts in one of the piles on the table. Perry realized that in addition to laundry, she must be offering mending as well. "There's a boarding house on the outskirts of the town limits, well beyond the mines. It's near a pub." She sighed and rested her needle on the fabric for a moment. "When Wilbur Stanley died in the mine cave-in, the family couldn't stay in the cottage no more. I found them a room at Sadie Calloway's. Now I wonder if I ought not to have stayed out of it. But there's no use looking over my shoulder at what's long past. They needed a place to live, and Katherine was in no shape to find one. Young Daisy was just six then, but she took on the role of head of the family. A good girl she was, a dear child. I tell you this much," she said, her eyes suddenly fierce, "if there was a man dead and blame fell on Daisy, she had a reason for it. She was a pretty thing. A man didn't have to be a sailor on shore to notice that. Katherine, well, she fell into a life of sin, no use in dressing it up as something else. Sadie said the fellows had begun noticing Daisy. She paid them no mind, of course, she was a good girl. But something happened. Sadie didn't know what. But all she heard from Katherine was that her sailor man was dead, and Daisy was to fault for it."

"But no one called the constable?"

Mrs. Larkin hesitated. "Folks who live their lives cutting corners off the commandments aren't quick to bring in the law," she said. "Sadie said no one was called and she'd have known.'

That didn't make sense. If there had been a murder, and Daisy's mother blamed Daisy, then surely she'd have gone to the police, if for vengeance itself.

"You're mighty curious," Mrs. Larkin noticed.

Perry realized that he needed to be more discreet. Mrs. Larkin was no fool.

"It just set me to thinking, that's all. You know how it is, there's not much diversion down in the mines. I thought today about what you'd said, and I got to wondering. Usually, when there's a murder done anywhere within fifty miles, everyone knows about it."

"That's so," Mrs. Larkin considered as she bit off the thread with her teeth. "I never heard a word of it until I talked to Sadie. I'd been planning to invite the Stanleys to my Annie's wedding, but when Sadie told me they'd all scarpered—leastways, the children, I didn't linger. I'm sorry to say it, but I'll not have a woman the likes of

Katherine Stanley at my daughter's wedding. I'd been wondering why the Stanleys weren't in church anymore. They'd been faithful for a long time, but long about June, they suddenly stopped coming. Now I know why, and it's a sad knowing. Daisy is a fine girl; I'd stake my hopes of heaven on that. I don't know what happened, but if that girl hangs for murder, there will be angels weeping above."

Mrs. Larkin's words set Perry to thinking. That night, as he lay asleep in the room that he'd previously shared with Daisy's three brothers, Perry considered his next move. If he could prove that Daisy was innocent, or at least that she had had cause for whatever had happened, he could possibly free her from the threat of the gallows. But first, he had to find out for himself what happened that night at the boarding house.

As he fell asleep, he couldn't help but wonder about the fate of the siblings. The Stanleys, Mrs. Larkin called them. Daisy hadn't even entrusted him with her real last name. Could he blame her, Perry thought realistically? He wondered where they were now.

∽

Vera agreed with Gerald. The old cottage where they'd dwelled with Perry wasn't as comfortable as the one on the Olsen estate, but it was far better than the abandoned mine.

"We know how to fetch what we need," she said confidently after the other sisters and brothers had settled down in their former rooms to sleep. "We can bring up some of what we had in the mine. The things are likely still there. We can get them tomorrow."

"I'll go to the farms around and seek work," Gerald said. "Harvest is over, so there's nothing to be had there. But animals still need to be fed, and stables need mucking out. I can do that."

The two nodded. It didn't seem as sure as when Daisy was with them, her faith and her resourcefulness finding a solution no matter how dire the circumstances. But they were together, and they weren't without options. They just needed to get through the winter.

"I hope Daisy is safe on her way to London," Vera said. "How long do you think it'll be until we have word of her?"

Gerald couldn't hazard a guess. He knew that after what had happened, Daisy's natural caution would make her hesitant to do anything that would reveal her whereabouts or that of her family. How could they know anything, he worried, when there was no way of finding out where she was? How would she find out where they were? Only God knew where they were. Daisy would have reminded them that God would find a way. Gerald reckoned that was so. All the same, he wished Daisy was still with them. She knew God better than any of them.

THE SCULLERY GIRL

Within a week of being in London, she was employed. She'd had no trouble finding work as a scullery maid; it wasn't work sought out by young girls with ambition, and since she'd appeared at the kitchen door with soot on her face, wearing a rumpled gray dress, the housekeeper had immediately hired her. There wasn't a fireplace in the maids' quarters upstairs on the third floor of the London estate where Daisy had found employment. But there was a roof over her head, and the leavings from the meals served to the Alcotts, and Daisy wasn't lazy.

Daisy kept to herself and was so quiet as she went about her work that the other maids were convinced she was simple-minded and, for the most part, they left her alone. She was too unkempt to catch the eye of the handsome footman, Theo, and she was no competition to Mary or

Gracie, the prettiest maids; therefore, she was not worth bothering.

On her Sunday half days, she went to church and stayed afterwards to pray for her siblings. For Perry, too, although she had to leave the words for that prayer in God's capable hands.

After the third Sunday, as the vicar was ready to leave the church when services had ended, he observed the shabbily dressed maid, her head bowed in prayer. His astute eyes took in her thin shawl, and he was moved to sympathy.

"My dear," he said in a gentle voice. "You are new to this part of London, I think?"

Daisy's head jolted up out of prayer. "Yes, Vicar," she said, exaggerating the northern accent so that she sounded as if she were a country girl new to the city.

"You're a young woman of piety, I see. You pray so steadfastly. For whom do you pray?"

"My family, Vicar," she told him. "I left them so that I could earn wages and send back, but I don't know where they are now, and they don't know where I am."

"I see. Where were they last?"

She hesitated. He was a vicar, and a man of God, but that did not guarantee the safety of her siblings.

He saw her reluctance to offer the information. "My dear," he said kindly, his lined face now smiling. "I will help if I can and do no harm. You have my word."

He was a man of God. She had to trust him. "They were in Oldham," she said.

The vicar's seamed features broadened into a wide smile. "Oldham," he said. "My wife's family lives there. She comes of farming stock. There are plenty of farms in Oldham. Farms and mines."

He patted her hand. "You let me pray on it, my dear, and we'll come up with a way for you to help them. But you might put some of your wages toward a warm coat for the winter," he advised.

Daisy shook her head. "I'm inside most of the time," she told him. "They'll need what I can give them more than I do."

The vicar doubted that this was so, but as she left the church, he watched her wrap the shawl tightly around her shoulders before she ventured outside. He bowed his head in prayer. There were so many in need. Perhaps he could help this one.

The following Sunday after church, Daisy stayed behind to pray as was her practice. The vicar came up to her and waited until she raised her head.

"I think we've found a way to help," he said. "My wife's nephew sends us things from the farm from time to time. He'll be coming up soon with meat from the fall slaughtering, He's a canny lad with a good heart. If you're willing, I'll have him bring a note to your family."

"I don't know where they are," she said.

"But you have an idea where they might be?"

Daisy hesitated. She suspected that her siblings would return to the familiar cottage where they'd first stayed after Perry brought them there. Gerald and Vera wouldn't want to risk being homeless in the bad weather. They'd likely move on when spring brought fair weather but for now, they'd not be wandering far.

"I think so."

"Good. You can write a note and send some money to them."

"Your wife's nephew . . . is he honest?" Daisy hated to ask such a question, but she didn't want to risk losing the money to a thief.

The vicar wasn't insulted. "Thomas is a good man," he assured her. "He keeps his thoughts to himself and no tittle-tattle. No thievery, too. He knows the Lord has been good to him and he's glad to do good to others."

Daisy decided to trust the vicar and hope that his nephew was as good as the vicar claimed.

"You write that note," the vicar said. "I'll send it off with your money for your family."

Daisy's face burned. "I—would you write it for me?" she asked humbly. "I don't have much learning."

Once again, the vicar found himself moved by this simple girl, with her honest eyes and shabby attire. "You have a wise heart, child," he said. "I'll write the note with the words you give me."

Daisy spent the week planning what the note should contain. She knew that it must not reveal too much, lest it put them in jeopardy. Most of the money they had insisted that she take with her was gone, spent in the journey to London, and she wanted to send them all that she had saved so they would have funds. But what if the nephew wasn't as honorable as his uncle seemed to think?

By the time she was in church the next Sunday, Daisy had made the decision to trust God and give her family everything she had saved. It was not much, but it was money they could use.

After services were over and the church had emptied out, the vicar led her into his office. There was a warm fire blazing, and he had a pot of tea and a plate of sandwiches.

"Those are from my wife," he said with a smile. "She always makes too much. She brings me lunch before she goes out to bring food to the members of our congregation who are in need. Won't you share them with me while I write your note? Now then," he said briskly before she had time to refuse. "You eat, and tell me what to write, and I'll be your scribe."

"Dear Gerald," Daisy dictated. "The vicar is sending his nephew, who has a farm in Oldham, to deliver this note. I am well and working. I have wages that his nephew will bring to you. I'll send more when I can. I pray that you are well and that you are saying your prayers. Your sister, Vera."

Daisy had decided that she would not use her own name. Her family would understand the reason for the subterfuge. She had deliberately only mentioned Gerald by name in the letter. There was nothing more she could do now but pray that the letter and the money reached their intended destination.

She was very busy in the kitchen at the Alcotts, for the Christmas season was approaching and the family did a lot of entertaining. Sometimes it seemed that she had no sooner finished washing up all the dishes and pans before they were dirtied from cooking and needed washing again. With guests coming and going, Daisy had the bedlinens to change, and the steps to keep clean of mud and dirt. By the time she had finished for the day, she was exhausted and fell into bed, too tired to even think.

When she learned that she would not be able to take her Sunday half-day because the Alcotts had family coming in from the country, Daisy was despondent. How would she know if the vicar's nephew had found her family and delivered the note and the money.

The kitchen maid and cook were not unsympathetic. It was always like this in the Alcott kitchen, Sarah told her. "They'll be going to see their kin in the country after Christmas; we'll get a break then."

Daisy nodded. She was lucky that Sarah was patient and the cook was good-tempered. Since going into service, she'd learned that scullery maids were often badly treated by the other servants as well as by the family. There was nothing to be done for it. She would have to wait until next Sunday to learn if her letter had been delivered.

∽

The vicar's nephew would not be the only one searching for the Stanleys. Perry, too, was spending his Sundays after church in search of his wife's family. The winds were cold, and darkness fell early, but Perry was determined to at least learn their whereabouts. He didn't need to make contact with them just yet, but he needed to know where they were.

He was walking along the road when he saw a wagon stopping in the vicinity of the abandoned mine. Intrigued by the sight, Perry concealed himself behind an old shed on the other side of the road and waited.

To his surprise, Gerald suddenly appeared from behind the height of a thick hedgerow and went to the wagon as if he knew the driver. The driver handed him what appeared to be a letter and a package. The two clasped hands, and then the driver of the wagon was on his way. Gerald, Perry observed, vanished for a bit but then Perry saw him again. He was walking as if he had a specific destination in mind.

Perry moved from behind the shed and walked stealthily among the trees, watching across the road. He could see Gerald for a bit, but then, when the hedges grew thick again, Gerald was once again out of sight.

But now it didn't matter, for Perry was certain that Daisy's family had taken refuge in the old cottage where Perry had lived when he first left his father's farm. Despite the cold wind and the threat of snow, Perry felt a sense of exultation. He had found Daisy's family. If they were getting letters, then likely they came from Daisy. Who else would be writing to them? Now it was up to him to find out the truth so that Daisy would be free from the threat of a murder charge. He would solve the mystery of the murdered man who appeared not to have died at all, and then, once Daisy's family knew he could be trusted, they would reveal where Daisy was.

He would have his wife and his family back again!

A VISIT WITH UNCLE IVOR

Perry attended the early service the following Sunday. He knew that he'd need more time if he was going to set his plan into motion. As soon as the service ended, Perry was on his way to Manchester. He'd sent a letter to his Uncle Ivor, asking if he could visit. Uncle Ivor had written back almost immediately, his delight in the message from his nephew coming through the very paper the words were written on.

It was a long walk, but Perry was accustomed to the exercise, and he didn't mind. It would be good to see Uncle again.

His uncle met him at the door of the big old farmhouse where he and his wife lived. Perry's cousins were grown now, with children of their own, and it was obvious that his uncle welcomed the company.

Perry's Aunt Millie had prepared a lot of food, and Perry was hungry enough to do the meal justice. "It's good to see a young man's appetite again," Aunt Millie declared.

"It's good to eat Welsh cooking again," Perry replied as he savored the taste of Welsh Cawl, which he hadn't eaten since his mother's death.

His aunt and uncle filled him in on the family events. It was good to hear about the Welsh side of the family. Perry didn't realize how much he'd missed their names until now. He was frank with his mother's relatives as he told them that he'd left the farm and told them why.

"You know, lad," Uncle Ivor said after they'd finished eating and he was filling his pipe for his after-the-meal smoke, "your grandfather is getting on in years. He'd like to have his own blood working the family farm."

"He's told you this?" Perry said in disbelief.

"Wrote it in a letter, he did. Mind you, the handwriting is not so easy to read, but the meaning was clear. My boys are English, they aren't leaving. But you now, you don't have a farm anymore." Uncle Ivor leaned forward. "Think it over. Now then, you've come here for a reason, and let's get to it."

Ivor Ellis was easy to talk to and easy to trust. He didn't blink an eye when Perry told him about Daisy, her mother, the incident at the boarding house that made Daisy believe she'd killed her mother's lover, and the mystery of why no one had been reported as dead to the authorities. As Perry talked, his uncle listened while small puffs of smoke came from his pipe. Aunt Millie refilled their cups with coffee and brought out dessert, Perry continued to explain.

"I have to prove she's innocent, Uncle Ivor. I handled it wrong, I know, and that's what drove her off. If I can prove that she didn't kill the sailor, she'll know that she doesn't have to live in hiding."

"She'll need to know why this sailor and her own mother want her to think she's a murderess," Ivor said. He took his pipe from his mouth and considered it in silence.

"Wickedness, that's what it is," Aunt Millie said, her voice raised in disbelief. "What sort of mother would speak against her own daughter?"

"Mrs. Larkin, the woman at church, seemed to think that Daisy's mother has just gone bad. But as long as Daisy thinks she murdered the sailor, she's not going to come back to me."

"Who could go to the boarding house without raising suspicion?" pondered Aunt Millie, who was as intrigued by the situation as her husband. She wiped crumbs away from the tablecloth. "That's where the answers are."

"The answers may be, but without finding the sailor, it's all for naught," Uncle Ivor said. He put his pipe back into his mouth and puffed on it. "Millie," he said after a time. "What's Gwillim up to these days?"

His wife looked at him. "Same as always. Resting out the winter until he takes to sea again. He makes a good income in the months when the weather is fine and takes his ease when it's cold."

"A good income, and the government never sees a penny of it," her husband remarked in a noncommittal tone. The puffs of smoke were coming out faster now, creating a cloud above Uncle Ivor's head. "Gwillim's always up for a lark," he said. "He's the one."

"The one to do what?"

"Why, to go to this boarding house and see about rounding up a crew for his ship.'

Perry didn't understand. "The sailor might already be at sea," he said.

"No matter," Uncle Ivor said calmly. "The other sailors will know who's on land and who's at sea. Gwillim's your man."

Uncle Ivor promised to speak to his friend Gwillim and see what they could set in motion. Aunt Millie wrapped up food for Perry to take home. She didn't like to see him leave, but she didn't want him walking in the dark and the cold.

"Mind, lad," Uncle Ivor said as the pair stood outside to bid Perry farewell, "you think on what I told you. It's a fine farm. You could do a lot worse. Good yields at harvest time, healthy livestock for breeding, a nice income from the sheep shearing, the farmhouse is big enough to raise a family," he said with a meaningful look, "it's well built, been standing for over 400 years and it's as stout as a fortress, the barn is big... you could do worse."

Once again, Perry had a lot to consider as he walked home. The difference was that, this time, he was eager to think of the possibilities that awaited if the plan worked. If this Gwillim chap was somehow able to find out more about the sailor who wasn't dead, that was all the proof that was needed to release Daisy from the fear of being apprehended.

He received a letter from his uncle less than a week later. Gwillim, who was indeed always up for a lark, it seemed, had agreed to play the part of a sea captain looking for likely lads to crew his boat when spring came. Nothing was more likely than to search the pubs; sailors who weren't at sea had a second home in the taverns around the docks. No suspicion would fall on Gwillim for playing a role, and if Perry wanted to be there, he'd be part of the ruse.

Perry sent back an answer agreeing to meet Gwillim at the pub by Sadie Calloway's boarding house on Thursday night. On Thursday afternoon, shortly after lunch, Perry began coughing. He'd never missed a day's work since coming to the mine, but he knew he'd need the time to get to the pub, linger there and stand a round of drinks to loosen the idle sailors' tongues, and then come back. It was worth the loss of wages if their actions this night could disprove Daisy's mother's accusation that her daughter was a murderess was a falsehood.

The night was clear and cold, and Perry was glad to see a fellow loitering outside the pub, scanning the road with an alert air.

"You Ivor's kin?" the man asked when Perry approached.

"His nephew, I am. Perry Dalton."

Gwillim was a man of middle years, old enough to captain a boat and know his way through the smuggling trade, and young enough to manage a rowdy crew whether it took fists or quick thinking. He had bright blue eyes, light hair so fair that it appeared white in the dark night, and the rolling gait of a man who, although he might indeed be wintering on land, was more used to the waves than the street.

Gwillim put out his hand. "Welcome then, Perry. I'll introduce you as my first hire."

Inside the pub, the air was thick with tobacco smoke. The fire was warm enough to ward off the chill of the December night. Gwillim strode up to the bar with a confident swagger. "I'm buying a drink for every man who's gone to sea and is looking for his next voyage come spring!" he roared.

There was a cheer from the men, clearly many of them sailors. Gwillim sat at a table close to the fire and far from the door. "Your uncle told me what I need to know," Gwillim said in a low voice as the bartender brought over a bottle. "I reckon we'll learn more about this dead sailor who's not been buried."

Perry was impressed by Gwillim's canny knack for questioning men on a matter which was not familiar.

"You know any others?" Gwillim asked when one of the early men eager to be recruited had already swallowed one sip and was eyeing the bottle with longing. "I'm looking for a man who's used to the sea. I don't want some green lad who has a notion to take to the water and ends up puking over the side."

The other man, a big, brawny, loose-limbed fellow whose arms and legs seemed to take up not only his chair but also the space on either side of it, laughed appreciatively. "Then you'll not want that yob you were just talking to," he said. "Talks like his grandfather fought with Nelson but knows no more of sailing than I know of running for Parleymint."

Gwillim guffawed at the jest. "That's what I mean now. If you're a man who doesn't mind a bit of a risk, then you're the man I need on my ship. Me and my crew, we don't exactly play by Royal Navy rules, if you get my drift."

The other fellow laughed even louder. "I'm for that, and what's more, I know another one or two who'll be happy to leave shore for a time."

Perry's instincts prickled at these words. Gwillim had played the other fellow perfectly by hinting at deeds that went afoul of the law.

Gwillim gave no indication that he had anything other than crewing his ship in mind. But he handed the bottle to the other man. "Go on, then, take a drink that shows me you're one who can handle his rum. Then tell me about any others who are of the same mind."

As the man began to talk, his tongue loosened by the free-flowing rum, Perry knew that Gwillim's tactics were working.

"He's likely over in the boarding house right now," the man, who introduced himself as Errol Dighe, told them in hushed tones. "Word is that he's dead, see, but some of us, we know better. Even the old lady what runs the boarding house don't know that he's there."

"Dead? What use is a dead man?"

"Ole Davy ain't dead, he just wants folks to think he is. I tell you this much," Errol said as he thrust his elbow into the air where he thought Perry's side would be, "the lady keeping him company knows he's not dead!"

"How's he hiding out in a boarding house if the landlady thinks he's dead?"

"Sadie Calloway likes her gin," was the answer. "Katie likes Davey well enough to keep him close by and no one the wiser. The wimmin who board there, well, they know how to keep their mouths shut. They're over here as often as they are in their beds." This set him to laughing uproariously.

"Why would a man who's pretending to be dead want to sail on my ship?"

"See, him making out to be dead is going to get him and Katie money. Katie's daughter thinks she killed him."

"I don't want mixed up in a murder," Gwillim said. "I'll turn a blind eye to most things, but I don't need any police looking into my business. I do enough to catch their attention as it is."

It was the right answer. As Errol talked, Perry felt a deepening disgust at the thought of how Daisy's mother could be party to a plan to extort money from her daughter, ostensibly to keep the supposed murder a secret, while the sailor, very much alive, profited from his lover's amorous deceit and his own culpability. Daisy was an innocent who had no chance to protest her innocence against such vile and reprehensible reprobates.

But now, with the truth revealed, Daisy's mother and her lover would soon be caught in their own machinations.

Gwillim gave Perry a wink when the sailor, overcome by the drink he had imbibed, laid his head on the table and was soon snoring. "Well, lad," he said softly. "Looks like we've found our man."

Perry reached into his pocket and pulled out the money to repay Gwillim for the cost of the rum, but the sea captain waved it away. "Winter is a dull time for a sailor like me," he said. "I've had myself a lark tonight. I should pay you!"

REUNION

Perry packed all his belongings into the wagon that his Uncle Ivor had lent him and then slapped the horse—also from Uncle Ivor—on its rump and set off for the old cottage where he knew the Stanley were living. He was on his way to Wales, to his grandfather's farm, and his grandfather had been made aware that Perry was bringing his family with him.

Although it was still winter, there was a late January thaw that had melted the snow, revealing the green underneath the covering of white. The sun, admittedly a rather pale version, was in the sky. It was as if God had decreed that this would be a benign day and Perry's spirits were high. He had food for the journey to Wales packed in a basket, enough for the six Stanleys and himself. He had the loan of a horse and a wagon for the trip. He had money saved up from frugal living. He also had articles that he'd clipped out from Manchester newspapers telling the story of a woman and her lover who had been arrested for attempted extortion.

The police had the testimony from Gwillim, who had told them what he'd learned from his evening at the pub. Errol Dighe had testified as well, although not willingly. Sadie Calloway had testified at the trial where Katherine and her sailor lover were sentenced to prison. They would not hang, but they would serve out their sentence. Perry had been in the courtroom when the verdict was pronounced. He wished that Daisy and her family could have been there, but he knew that they would not have taken the risk of showing themselves publicly, even in such a setting.

Perry also knew, as he pulled on the reins so that the horse would take the signal and turn down into the valley where the old cottage was located, that the Stanleys would not be easy to convince. The newspaper clippings were his proof.

He pulled up to the cottage and sprang from the wagon. The cottage looked deserted, but Perry knew that was intentional. He knew that behind the curtains, all of Daisy's brothers and sisters would be watching to see why he was there.

The door, he knew, would be locked. He didn't try the doorknob. He knocked on the door and waited.

Everything inside was still, contributing to the impression that no one was at home.

Perry sensed otherwise. "Gerald!" he called. "Vera! I've got a wagon and a horse so that we can go to London and fetch Daisy."

Nothing, not a stirring from within. Yet, he sensed an alertness that was borne as much out of curiosity as wariness.

"I know that you know where she is," he went on. "I saw you, Gerald, when you met with that fellow who brought you a letter."

He waited. Still nothing.

Perry pulled one of the newspaper articles from his pocket. "The police aren't hunting for Daisy," he said. "The sailor isn't dead. He was never dead at all. It was a plot to try to trick Daisy into paying your mother money to keep her from telling the authorities that Daisy had killed him. But he wasn't dead."

Perry slid the article under the door, through the crack that always let in a draft in the cold weather. From within, he could hear the slightest indication of movement.

He waited to give them time to read it, to question if it was reliable, to make the decision whether or not to trust him. They were used to living in quiet from their days in the mine and then at the cottage. The freedom of living in the cottage at the Olsen estate must have been nothing but a frail memory for them now.

Slowly, the door opened. Gerald and Vera came out.

Gerald had matured. There was stubble on his chin now; he hadn't been shaving yet when he and his siblings left in the autumn. Vera was taller. Thinner, too, with sharp blue eyes that looked at him with distrust.

"I'm sorry," he said at once. "I never meant for you to be separated from Daisy. I—"

"Is this true?" Vera demanded, holding up the clipping.

"Of course, it's true. I have more, from other newspapers. Your mother is in prison for her crime. She'll have to serve her sentence. So will the sailor. Daisy has nothing to fear."

Vera came up to him. "If you're lying to us, and if this is a trick to trap Daisy, I warn you, Perry Dalton—"

"It's no trick. I've come for you. I borrowed a wagon and horse from my uncle. I've packed what I own, and you need to bring all of your belongings. We're wasting time. We're going to get Daisy. Then we're going to Wales. My grandfather is expecting us. He wants me to take over the farm that's been in our family for centuries. I told him I'm bringing my wife and my family with me."

The door slowly opened and the other Stanleys came out. Eva didn't disguise her pleasure at seeing him. Morris and Gus ran to him. "Did you say we're going to see Daisy?" Morris asked.

"As soon as you lot can get your things in the wagon!"

It took less time for the Stanleys to load their possessions into the wagon than it had taken for Perry to convince them to open the door. Vera and Gerald sat in the wagon seat with Perry; the younger Stanleys were ensconced in the back of the wagon amidst their belongings.

Knowing that they were probably hungry, Perry told Vera that he'd packed a basket with food for all of them. As they set off for London, the younger children were giggling as if they were set on a great adventure. Gerald and Vera didn't have much to say at first, but Perry could sense that they were both excited and fearful. So, as the horse ambled its way along the road that would take them to London, he told them about the way that he had discovered, with Gwillim's help, the truth about what happened that night. They listened attentively as they ate their bread and cheese. He was surprised that they didn't have many questions to ask. Except one, repeatedly.

"Is Daisy truly safe now?"

He showed them the other clippings, all rendering the same account.

He felt sorry for them, having to absorb so much tribulation in their young lives. They needed something to cheer them up.

"We're going to be a farming family," he said. "There's plenty of work to do, but it'll be our farm and no one will make us leave it. We'll take care of the fields and the animals, and we'll keep what we earn. No one will hurt you there. Daisy will be with us."

～

Gerald had the address for the vicar, who was astonished to see them. Then he invited them in.

"You must be weary," he said as he opened his door. Inside, the fire crackled invitingly, and the leftover aromas from breakfast were tantalizing. "Come inside and rest up from your journey. London is quite a distance!"

"Thank you, sir, but we're in a hurry," Perry said. "We want to see Daisy."

The vicar understood. "Of course, you do," he said with a wide smile. "If there's room for me on that seat, I'll show you where she's working. Alice," he called into the house, "I'm going out, I shan't be long."

Used to the unexpected, the vicar's wife bid him a cheery goodbye as she brought him his coat and hat. Then he climbed into the wagon seat. It was a tight squeeze, but they managed to fit. Perry handed him the reins.

"We're on our way to Wales," Gus said proudly from the back of the wagon.

"Wales! You have another journey ahead."

"Yes, sir," Vera answered. "But we're going home."

"All of us," Gerald added. "With our Daisy. I mean Vera," he corrected himself guiltily.

The vicar smiled but gave no sign that he had noticed anything amiss. He drove the wagon into a section of London with elegant houses and tree-lined streets. Ladies with stylish bonnets and fur muffs walked briskly, arm-in-arm with fine gentlemen. He stopped the wagon in front of an imposing house set back from the street and enclosed within a wrought iron fence.

"I'll fetch her, shall I?" the vicar said as if he knew that the Alcott butler would not allow Daisy/Vera to receive visitors at the front door.

They saw the door open, and the vicar stepped inside. The Stanleys waited in front of the house, all of them, even Perry, anxious. For Daisy's siblings, it was an anxiety that came out of the dreadful ache of missing her. For Perry, the feelings were deeper. When he had last seen Daisy, he had believed her guilty of murder. It was that wrenching event that had led to the uncovering of the truth, but would that be enough? Would she forgive him? Would she be willing to stay married to him, to entrust him with the care of her and her family, and to relocate to Wales?

It seemed forever before the grand front door opened and the vicar stepped out. Daisy, wrapped in a thin shawl with a battered hat on her head, was at his side. He bent down to say something to her and the loved ones waiting in the wagon saw her nod.

Then she began to run toward them. Her hat fell from her head but she didn't bother to stop to pick it up from the ground. She was running, her face alive as none of them remembered seeing it. Her black hair flowed behind her as the pins holding it in place followed the hat to the ground.

Perry handed the reins to Gerald. "Hold these," he said.

Gerald looked uneasy. "What if he bolts?"

"He won't," Perry said as he jumped down from the wagon seat. In three long strides he was at the gate. Daisy ran into his open arms and he lifted her up.

She was laughing. "The vicar said not to wait for him, he'll get a ride back from one of the grooms. He said we're going to Wales!"

"You're willing?" Perry said, his voice pleading. "You'll forgive me, and you'll be my wife, and we'll be a family?"

"Oh, yes," Daisy exclaimed. A decade of worry had magically been erased from her face and her eyes were vivid with joy. He had never seen her this way.

He put her down on the ground and then, not caring that five sets of eyes were watching, he lowered his lips to hers.

"Well, Mrs. Daisy Dalton," he said softly, pressing his fingers where his lips had just been, "are you willing to be a farmer's wife?"

Daisy flung her arms around him. "I'm willing for whatever comes our way," she promised. She held up her hand to show him her ringless finger. "I can wear it again," she said. "I've kept it safe all this time, trusting that God would make things right."

Perry picked her up and carried her to the wagon, returning her to the family who had missed her so terribly. There would be time for more hugs and kisses, and more telling to be done along the journey. Daisy Dalton and the rest of his family were finally going home.

∽

THANK YOU FOR CHOOSING A PUREREAD BOOK!

We hope you enjoyed the story, and as a way to thank you for choosing PureRead we'd like to send you this free book, and other fun reader rewards...

Click here for your free copy of Whitechapel Waif
PureRead.com/victorian

Thanks again for reading.
See you soon!

We also have a little treat for you on the following pages. PureRead enjoys the privilege to work with many authors. One of our newest arrivals is Jess Weir.

We would like to introduce you to her first novel published with PureRead, The Midwife's Dream. Over the page you can read the first chapter of the book, following the harrowing story of Kathryn Barton and her journey to her own very special happy ever after...

INTRODUCING JESS WEIR

THE MIDWIFE'S DREAM

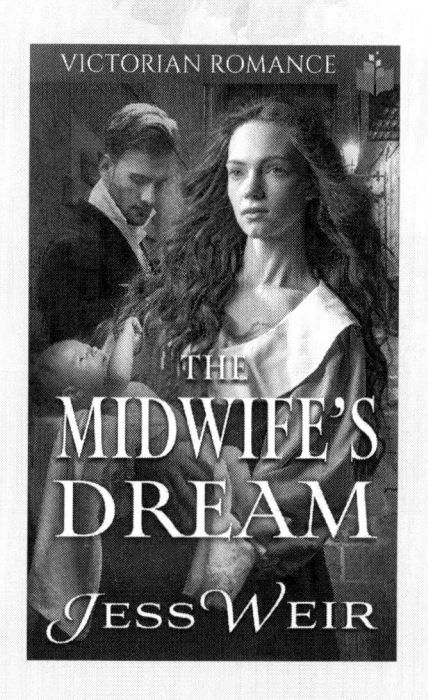

Kathryn Barton dreams of becoming a midwife. In Victorian London, dreams have a nasty habit of turning into nightmares...

"You look a little pale today," Kathryn Barton said as she reached out to lay her hand on her mother's forehead. "You're perspiring, are you..."

"Kathryn, stop! It's not polite to point out such things, what if your father heard you?" Beth Barton was in the last weeks of her confinement. With a look that bordered on fear, she peered over Kathryn's shoulder as if her husband might appear at any moment.

"Papa is at work," Kathryn said and laughed. "If he isn't concerned for his wife's health, then the shame is his, not mine."

"Kathryn! You mustn't!" Beth's voice had dropped to a whisper.

"He's in the city, Mama."

"But your sister is not!" Beth hissed. "You will upset her by saying such things about your father."

"Very well, but I still think you're pale and clammy. I think I ought to call the doctor."

"You know what your father will say. He doesn't like you learning this sort of thing."

"I'm going to have to learn such things if I want to be a nurse, aren't I?"

"You are just fourteen; there's time enough for you to think about such things in the future."

Beth was a little dismissive and it hurt Kathryn. She knew her father couldn't care less about educating women for work in any way, shape, or form, but she had thought her own mother might be on her side, at least in private.

"I'm hungry, Mama!" Jane, just twelve years old, sauntered listlessly into the room.

"Have you finished the work Miss Marlon gave you?" Beth asked in a tone that was more indulgent than it was stern.

"Yes," Jane said and sighed. "Although, I don't see the point."

"The point of being at least a little educated?" Kathryn scoffed; she and her younger sister were like chalk and cheese. Two more different sisters could hardly be found in all of London.

"When I'm married, I won't need to know how many degrees make up a triangle. Who even cares about such things?"

"Education is a privilege, Jane." Kathryn shook her head in exasperation. The sisters had had this same argument time and time again, with neither one giving an inch.

"For you, perhaps." Jane snorted with laughter. "Since no man will ever marry you!"

"If it's a man who wants an ill-educated woman, then I would sooner never be married!"

"Just as well!" Jane stuck out her tongue and then turned her nose up, signalling that she had won.

"Girls!" Beth's voice raised. "I'm tired and I cannot cope with your constant arguing." Already, their mother was walking away, heading for the stairs.

This was a signal that Beth was going to lay down on her bed. Lately, it seemed like it was all she ever did. Kathryn loved her mother dearly, but she often secretly wished that the woman had just a little more spirit. Of course, she was heavy with child and her fatigue was entirely understandable. However, with child or not, this seemed to be Beth Barton's way of doing things. She retreated. She gave in. She never, ever fought.

"Mama, I do wish you'd let me fetch the doctor," Kathryn persisted.

"And what would your father say?" Beth paused, her foot already on the bottom step. "He would remind you that we are not made of money!"

"We are far from poor, Mama." Kathryn shook her head. Her father's little sayings were both patronising and irritating to her.

"Because your father is careful with his money. He works hard, we cannot fritter away the proceeds of that hard work." And with that, Beth continued up the stairs.

The words were not her own, a fact which irritated Kathryn all the more. She'd heard these things word for word from her father's lips almost daily, year after year. He acted as if his own family were draining him. As if they had no right to be fed and clothed and live under his roof, even if that roof had only become his as a result of his marriage to Beth.

Still, her mother and Jane seemed to idolise him, for all the good it did them, for he no more favoured them than he did Kathryn, his errant daughter who insisted on thinking for herself. Kathryn, for her part, was glad to receive no favour from him. He was a selfish man who, in her opinion, if not her mother's and sister's, was entirely dissatisfied with his life. If ever a man regretted his choice of wife or the fact that his only children were female, it was Warren Barton.

"I'm still hungry," Jane said, but it was quietly spoken, not meant for their careworn mother's ears.

"Go down to the kitchen and speak to Mavis," Kathryn said, trying to let go of their differences for a moment. "She'll give you some bread and butter to keep you going until lunch." Jane smiled and nodded before disappearing from the room, leaving Kathryn alone.

Kathryn picked up the book she'd been reading the day before and sat down on the comfortable chintz-covered couch with a sigh. She was too distracted to read, but she opened the book to the correct page before setting it down on her lap. She seemed to be the only member of the household who was worried about her mother. Even Beth herself seemed not to care about her own health, as if she really were no more than a piece of equipment; a manufacturing unit producing babies, *or not,* as was so often the case.

Beth Barton had conceived no less than seven times to Kathryn's certain knowledge. All seven had been female, and only two of them survived. Kathryn wondered if her mother carried the much-coveted male now, or if a healthy child was to be just another female-shaped disappointment for her father.

She had come to despise the man who had arbitrarily decided that his entire family was pointless without a son. And if her mother managed to birth a healthy baby this time, and a male, no less, Kathryn wondered how she would feel about the helpless baby boy.

Would he grow up to be arrogant and dismissive? A chip off the old block, learning his habits and snarling opinions from his father? Or would he be his very own man? A fine man who would love and care for his mother and sisters, treating them as beloved, always listening, understanding, and never, ever assuming himself to be their better. Kathryn snorted, knowing the latter to be almost entirely unlikely.

"Poor Mama," Kathryn said quietly in the darkness.

"And poor Papa," Jane added, making sure that their father was protected, even amongst themselves in the dead of night.

"I hadn't realised you were still awake," Kathryn said, wishing she hadn't spoken aloud in the first place. She was listening to the arguing voices drifting through the still of the night, trying to make out the words through the deadening insulation provided by the walls of their three-story terraced house.

"How could anyone sleep through Mama's crying?" Jane said without a hint of caring or respect for their mother.

"Then perhaps Papa shouldn't be so cruel as to make her cry," Kathryn snapped back, irritated by her sister's ever-present position of coming down on their father's side. She sometimes thought of her mother and sister as whipped dogs, eager to do anything to please their master. Well, Kathryn would never be anybody's whipped dog, never!

"He just wants a son, Kathryn. Is that too much for a man to ask?"

"You are parroting his words, Jane. Do you never listen to yourself when you speak? Do you never wonder how it is Mama feels when she is so berated?"

"Other women have sons, Kathryn."

"At twelve you are so sure of life, aren't you?" Kathryn said, employing a little of her father's derision and noting how Jane bridled. So, she would only stand it from their father, would she? "How do you imagine you might feel one day to be in Mama's shoes? To have lost so many babies is heart-breaking for a woman, and certainly not something she should be blamed for."

"I didn't say she should be blamed for that!"

"Oh, but she should be blamed for giving birth to girls? Really! Listen to what you're suggesting and try to educate yourself." Kathryn was angry now. How could they be so different? "If you understood anything at all of simple biology, then you would know that there is no way for anybody, man or woman, to ensure the sex of a child in the womb."

"The way you speak!" Jane made rather a good job of pious outrage. "If Papa heard you speak that way, he would punish you!"

"Biology is a fact of life, Jane. Understanding it might well spare you some agony in your future. It might make your choice of a husband something you think about very carefully, for one thing."

"Are you suggesting our father is not a good man?" Jane always fell on distraction when she had no sensible answer.

"No, I'm not. I'm not suggesting it, I'm saying it outright!"

"You selfish, ungrateful girl!"

"Again, you are parroting his words, Jane, learn to think for yourself."

"Why? So that I can be like you?" Jane scoffed. "So that I can read unsuitable textbooks and think myself clever? And for what? To end up as a nurse at St Thomas'? No, thank you!"

"You speak as if there's something shameful in it!"

"Shameful or not, Papa will never allow it, so who's the real fool here?" Jane's cruel, sharp tongue was well developed for a girl of just twelve.

"Go to sleep, Jane," Kathryn said with a sigh and covered her head with her feather pillow. Jane continued to talk, but Kathryn couldn't hear it. What was the point of conversation in such a house?

Still, Jane's words had cut her deeply, for there was some truth in them. Truth, at least, in her declaration that their father would never allow Kathryn to follow her dream of becoming a nurse.

Warren Barton was a curious mixture of conflicting ideas, but not uncommon in his contradictions. Like so many other men of their class, he chose to bemoan his lot, to belittle his family for the fact that he alone was the breadwinner. At the same time, his aspirations were so great that the idea of his daughters choosing a vocation of their own, of bringing some money into the household, was anathema to him.

How could a girl in such a household ever win? Perhaps Jane was right; perhaps Kathryn really was the fool. Jane was playing the game, never in conflict, always with her toe right on the line. Kathryn's determination to be herself, to follow her own dreams, to treat her life as her very own, she was forced to admit, caused her an endless amount of suffering.

Kathryn was always fighting, even though she fought in silence. She was always planning, always trying to escape the fear, the certain knowledge, that all her planning was in vain. Wasn't she just, in the end, making her own life miserable?

Knowing that she wouldn't sleep, Kathryn came out from beneath the pillow. Jane was mercifully silent, although likely still awake herself.

"You are no sort of woman at all!" Kathryn heard her father's voice clearly and winced at the thought of her mother having to suffer his abuse. "For if you were truly a woman, a real woman, I would already have a son. I strongly suggest, if you know what's good for you, that you provide me with a healthy son this time, Beth."

Kathryn blinked back her tears, for they would be of little use. No wonder her sister thought that the sex of a child could be decided at will if their own father espoused such views. She hardly knew whether to pity her sister for being so blind or to be angry with her for being so determined to believe such a thing.

More than anything, however, Kathryn wondered what would happen if her mother gave birth to another baby girl.

The thought of sending a prayer up to Heaven crossed Kathryn's mind, but she quickly dismissed it. Even if she wanted to pray, she had no idea how to. Among the many strong ideas and 'principals' that her father had, the strongest was the belief that going to church was for weak people. "If people need a thing above to rule over them, they'll never get to a place where they can rule themselves." He'd say with an arrogant nod of his head. Kathryn felt deep down that he was wrong, that maybe having a God to look over them could make them into stronger more secure people, but there was nothing she could do. And so, she had never once set foot in a church, and her father's insidious apprehension against anything to do with it seeped into her own outlook on the world, almost subconsciously.

Whatever the reasons for it may have been, Kathryn didn't send a prayer up to God. All she could do was roll onto her other side and try and get some sleep…

To continue reading pick up your copy of The Midwife's Dream by Jess Weir on Amazon

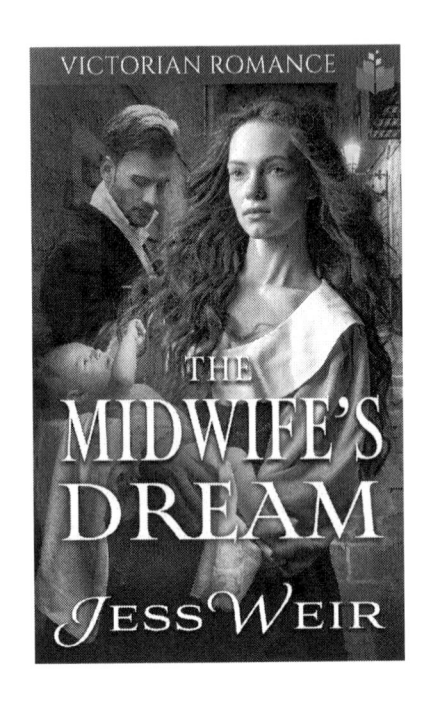

Click here to search Midwife's Dream Jess Weir

LOVE VICTORIAN ROMANCE?

If you enjoyed this story why not continue straight away with other books in our PureRead Victorian Romance library?

Read them all...

Victorian Slum Girl's Dream

Poor Girl's Hope

The Lost Orphan of Cheapside

Born a Workhouse Baby

The Lowly Maid's Triumph

Poor Girl's Hope

The Victorian Millhouse Sisters

Dora's Workhouse Child

Saltwick River Orphan

Workhouse Girl and The Veiled Lady

OUR GIFT TO YOU

AS A WAY TO SAY THANK YOU WE WOULD LOVE TO SEND YOU THIS BEAUTIFUL STORY FREE OF CHARGE.

Click here for your free copy of Whitechapel Waif

PureRead.com/victorian

At PureRead we publish books you can trust. Great tales without smut or swearing, but with all of the mystery and romance you expect from a great story.

Be the first to know when we release new books, take part in our fun competitions, and get surprise free books in your inbox by signing up to our free VIP Reader list.

As a welcome gift you'll receive the story of the Whitechapel Waif straight to your inbox...

Click here for your free copy of Whitechapel Waif

PureRead.com/victorian

Printed in Great Britain
by Amazon